THE BIRD FLIES TO GOD

THE BIRD FLIES TO GOD

Kacy Curtis

iUniverse, Inc.
New York Lincoln Shanghai

The Bird Flies to God

iUniverse books may be ordered through booksellers or by contacting:

iUniverse
2021 Pine Lake Road, Suite 100
Lincoln, NE 68512
www.iuniverse.com
1-800-Authors (1-800-288-4677)

ISBN-13: 978-0-595-35048-3 (pbk)
ISBN-13: 978-0-595-67191-5 (cloth)
ISBN-13: 978-0-595-79754-7 (ebk)
ISBN-10: 0-595-35048-8 (pbk)
ISBN-10: 0-595-67191-8 (cloth)
ISBN-10: 0-595-79754-7 (ebk)

Printed in the United States of America

PART I

▼

CHAPTER 1

▼

I BEG TO DIFFER

SWEETHEART

Fresh out of the corps and already my life is mangled beyond all recognition. In Korea on those long sweaty nights when the mountains threaten to swallow me whole and shit out my bones in the shape of a grave I dream about the states. But now that I'm back I already miss the simplicity of combat. A group of men I can trust my life with and an enemy who opposes my existence. It's easy. It makes sense. I don't have to think. But back here in the states it's nothing but thinking. It's all one big puzzle and I'm the piece that doesn't seem to fit right.

It's the enemy that gives me my ticket out of that dirty little war. Some slant-eye's handiwork. Blanchard is a member of my platoon. A corn-fed white boy from the mid west. He has a thick neck. A crew cut. A square jaw. Shoulders like a mountain gorilla's. He was defensive end for the University of Oklahoma before joining the marines and every night in the mountains he keeps me up with all the reasons he should be playing for the Colts instead of risking his neck for a bunch of ungrateful Americans. In the end his fate is the same as if he had managed to go pro. Although it isn't an offensive tackle that gives him bum knees. It's a landmine. He doesn't see it. Nobody sees it. We just hear the click then the boom. Along with a little shrapnel in my side I get a thank-you letter from Uncle Sam and a ticket out of that useless country. Blanchard gets two sticks of jerky where he used to have legs and a wheelchair for the rest of his days.

I want my arrival to surprise Susan so I don't mention my discharge in the letters I write from the hospital. I touch down in Los Angeles five weeks later on a Friday night. I spend the weekend with a herd of drunken jarhead pussy-hounds. We're all fresh out of the war and thirsty for mayhem American style. I chase tail purely for sport. Not looking to close the deal. Just rolling wing-man to help the guys get action. We hit every hop-head pad on Hollywood Boulevard. Pool halls. Jazz joints. Honky-tonks. Negro dance halls. Any dive with booze and broads we're there. We're all crazy from combat and still have that bad juju blood sizzling in our brains. The weekend passes in a blur. Neon signs. Tiki-torch shacks with bamboo facades. Wild dames with tight skirts and star spangled eyes. Drag races. Fist fights.

Monday morning is a set of brass knuckles and I find myself in a cheap hotel. I reek of whiskey and look like something death carries with him in a suitcase. I can hear a couple of winos retching in the john at the end of the hall. A prostitutes head is banging against the wall and I think the whole damn place is going to come down.

It's a filthy weekend. It's just what I needed. But it's time to clean up my act. I shave my face and wash the stink of debauchery off then catch a cab to my girlfriend's place.

She rents a cute two bedroom stucco cottage in the Hollywood hills and as the taxi rolls to a stop in front of her place I can see the whole valley sprawled out below. The taxi splits and I stand there feeling funny. My legs are weak and the moths are in my gut doing their love-bird dance. I gulp in the warm California air then fly up the front steps and knock on the door. I'm dolled up in uniform and ready to knock her socks off. I want to see her big baby blues light up. I want to hear her shrill laughter. I want to feel her nails digging into my back. I want to ditch all my gory war luggage in the pockets of her love. I want to relish in the freedom that I've spent eighteen months fighting for.

She doesn't answer the door. I leak a sad sigh and try the knob. It's unlocked. I step inside and make myself at home. The place is just like I remember. Hardwood floors. Vaulted ceiling. Breakfast nook. A snazzy joint for a gal her age.

I'm pouring a glass of juice when I hear something in the bedroom. It sounds like a puppy getting strangled to death. All shrieks and gurgles and yelps. When I push open Susan's bedroom door my jaw hits the floor. I can't believe my eyes. Some dago looking prick with a bad mustache and too much back hair is on top of the bed. Susan is beneath him. Her ankles by her ears. The wop is gripping his dick like a switch-blade and jamming it into her gaping corn-hole. Susan's face is contorted with ecstasy. She looks half way retarded. The emotion I feel is a lack of all emotions. I stand silent and empty and numb. I watch my girlfriend take it in the ass like a two-bit junky whore and all I feel is nothing. I turn to leave and that's when they hear me.

"What the hell? Fucking pervert" he yells.

"Buckley it's not what it looks like" Susan cries. "I can explain."

"You know this peeping-tom asshole" he asks?

"He's my boyfriend" she says.

"Well I don't give a rat's ass who he is. Nobody barges in on me like this."

He comes at me like a Billy goat. Stark raving naked. His dirt-covered sundial still at half mast. I swing first. I always swing first. It's a clean punch. Hard. Fast. Full of bad intentions. His head jerks back. His jaw goes cock-eyed. I hear his teeth crack. He drops to his knees. I continue to throw. I want to dismantle his face. I want to yank his spine out through his mouth. I'm not mad at him. I'm mad at myself for not caring. I'm mad at the war for what it has done to me. He's just in the wrong place at the wrong time. I pick up the radio from Susan's dresser and hoist it over my head.

"Buckley stop" she pleads. "It's not his fault. Put it down."

I throw the radio onto his face. His legs twitch. Blood spreads out on the hardwood floor.

"What the hell are you doing Buckley?"

"What" I ask? "I put it down didn't I?"

"Oh you are a fucking ass-hole."

"I beg to differ sweet heart. From where I was standing it looked like this hairy dago was the only one fucking asshole around here."

I light a Lucky Strike and walk outside.

The next morning I drop a pretty penny on a used car. A 1946 Cadillac with a black paint job and curves like a math teacher I wanted to bang in high school. I stuff all my belongings in the trunk and lay a trail of rubber down the center of my shattered dreams. As I race out of Los Angeles I don't look back. I know the city is watching me. Watching me with that smoggy red sun. That sore swollen eye.

Nineteen hours later I'm outside of El Paso in the middle of the night. Except for gas and the occasional greasy spoon I haven't stopped driving. I'm pushing my Caddy with a stupid fury. The stars overhead are chasing me but they didn't stand a chance. My appetite for speed is insatiable. Like some puss-faced Venice Beach bum with a bottle of cheap booze. The more I consume the more I need. I don't have a plan. I just know the longer I keep moving the less I have to think.

When I reach the Atlantic it will be time to stop. I plan on building a new life out there. I've never seen New York.

But that will all come later. It's time now for adrenaline and bitterness and speed and regret. I can see the deceit in the letters she wrote. I can see her on that bed. Bent like a flimsy doll. I can feel the mountains still threatening to eat my soul. I can see the eyes in the darkness and hear the artillery fire. I can feel the war and the death and the cheating all around me.

I begin to cry. It's the first time I've cried since I shot that old woman near the Changjin reservoir. But it's worse than that. It's all the tragedies life has thrown my way. It's the early death of my parents. It's the look on Susan's face when she saw me in the doorway. It's the way the blood poured from that peasant woman's left eye socket. It's the sadness of a Texas highway at night.

On the radio is Charlie Parker playing "Easy to Love." I turn it up loud and keep pushing down the highway hoping to out run the pain. Clouds start spreading across the sky. The stars die one by one. Along with the darkness comes the rain. It comes unexpectedly like a right hook from someone you thought was your friend. The drops hammer against the windshield in perfect time with the Parker tune. Lightening rips across the sky. The thunder is not far behind. Growling. Rumbling. Screaming. It chases it's creator across the darkened landscape.

Suddenly tail-lights appear about a hundred yards ahead. I lay on the brakes and drop my speed down to something close to legal. I'm thinking about how to pass when its rear tires fish-tail across the wet highway. Water sprays into the air. It's red from the glow of the tail-lights and looks like blood spewing from a severed limb. The car skids down the middle of the road then hits the gravel shoulder and flips. It rolls as effortlessly as a tumbleweed in a dry wind.

I skid to a stop and stare in dismay as the crumpled piece of metal comes to a violent halt in a nearby field. I kill the engine. All is silent save the pitter-patter of rain drops on the windshield. I open the car door and step out into the storm.

I don't believe that someone could be alive inside that ball of metal and glass but as I approach I hear a voice. It's a ragged broken ugly voice. I crouch beside the wreck. Just then a dagger of lightening flashes across the sky allowing me to glimpse the horror inside the car. It's a man. No. It used to be a man. Now it's just a tasteless joke with a crooked mouth. He's old and there's blood all over his face. I begin tugging at the door.

"Come on" I yell. "We're getting you to a hospital."

"I'm not going anywhere" he growls with a throat full of gore.

"Bull shit" I say. "We're getting you out of here."

"Don't kid yourself. Take a look at me."

Then as if on cue the lightening flashes again. I look in at his mangled face. His glasses are shattered giving him a hundred jagged eyes. His mouth is a dripping gash. I can only imagine the steering wheel is responsible for robbing him of his pearly whites. He begins to speak. This time his words are preceded by a bloody bubble.

"A man knows when it's his time" he says. "Nobody can save me now."

"If you think I'm going to let you die here you got another thing coming."

"Do you really want to help me" he asks?

"Yes" I reply. "Just tell me what I can do."

"Really" he asks?

"Yes. What?"

"You can finish what I set out to do" he says.

"And what's that?"

"In the trunk you'll find a briefcase" he says with blood seeping from his broken mouth. "That briefcase needs to be in Shreveport Louisiana by tomorrow night. There's a warehouse across from the docks. 415 Emerick Street. Be there at midnight."

"What's in the briefcase" I ask?

"You don't want to know" he says. "Just be by the docks at midnight. 415 Emerick Street."

"Maybe this isn't a good idea" I stammer.

"Promise me."

"What's your name" I ask franticly?

"The docks" he whispers. "Midnight."

And just like that it ends. He takes his last breath. I watch his old yellow eyes roll upside down. His toothless mouth hangs agape. Blood trickles from his ears. His nose is wide open. He resembles all the other sorry saps I've seen strewn across this pitiless earth. Death looks the same wherever you go. It's a dead-end street and it doesn't matter if you're driving a Studebaker or a Rolls Royce.

An hour later I'm hunkered down at the bar in some shady road-side tavern tossing back a shot of rye. Hank Williams blares from the juke box. I have a head-ache like a possum's digging around inside my skull.

The bartender is dressed just like everybody else. Boots. Levis. A shirt that resembles a tablecloth my grandma used to put out every Fourth of July. He's a tall drink of water. Skinny as a rail. And with the ten gallon hat perched on his mug he comes off looking like a six foot nail.

"Keep them coming slim" I demand.

"Maybe you should catch your breath mister."

"Thanks mom" I say slamming a dollar on the bar. "But I know how to handle my liquor."

"Whatever you say boss" he grumbles as he pours another shot and walks off scowling.

I toss it back and stroll over to the jukebox. I drip rain water across the floor and catch evil eyes from the red-necks shooting stick. The honky-tonk is killing me. I need something to help me think. I need some jazz. I find an old soothing number from Sinatra and drop in a nickel. The record kicks on and Frank's voice is a little piece of magic. All the cow-pokes look bent out of shape but I don't care. The horns are smooth and sweet and my thoughts start flowing like neon rain through the gutters of the night.

How has this all come about? Why am I in Texas in the middle of the night? Why did I take a stranger's briefcase if it's locked and I have no idea what's inside? Is it fate? Is it destiny? No. Fate's a scapegoat for sissies and yellow bellies. And destiny's just a cross-eyed drag queen with a smoke-stained wig and bad teeth. But what then? What else is there?

I'm desperate to place blame on someone other than myself. But I know better than that. I'm the one who dropped the nickel in the jukebox and I'm the one who has to dance to the music. But why are my pockets so full of loose change? Why do I keep shoving coins into this stupid machine? What is it I'm searching for? Had I felt it in the arms of that two-timing whore? Had I expected to find it on the battlefields of Korea? Will I find it on the east coast? Is it locked inside the briefcase? Will I even know it if I find it?

In this the year of our Lord 1951 we are given the American dream only one fragment at a time. But it's out there just the same. I know it. And it's up to us to gather it up. I heard it once on a Louis Armstrong album. I saw it hiding between the lines of a Jack London novel. I felt it in the roar of the crowd when DiMaggio crushed the game winning homer.

But everybody finds their dreams in different places. My dream isn't to be found in classrooms or offices or stuffy restaurants. My dream is waiting out in the gutters and the shadows. It's in the alleys and the bars and the all night diners. It's on the dark highways. It's in the smoke. It's in the whispers. It's out there somewhere and I plan on finding it.

I crush my Lucky in the ashtray and head out to sleep in my Cadillac. I'm going to need some shut-eye if I plan on driving to Shreveport tomorrow.

CHAPTER 2

▼

AND THE CADILLAC IS PURRING LIKE A FAT LAZY FARM CAT

I'm rolling past Fort Worth about eleven in the morning when I start thinking about women. I think about the way they smell after sex in the rain with Old Crow and Chesterfield's still on their breath. I think about the way they can blush and giggle on a bed of red satin with a stiff cosmopolitan in one hand and a dirty pulp fiction dime novel in the other. I think about the sound that is made when their grey wool skirts rub against their stockings. I think about women and sex and the origin of desire.

I spit in my palm and shove my hand down my pants. My cock feels like a steel rod. I let my mind wander. I envision a Puerto Rican school girl sitting on the seat beside me. Her short plaid skirt is ridding up. Her dark legs are shiny and smooth. She is staring at me with these large green eyes that seem to convey some brilliant filthy haiku about lip-stick and gin. She unzips my pants and pulls out my cock. Her eyes light up like a child who has found a toy in the street. Leaning over my lap she opens up and takes me inside her mouth. It's warm and wet. I grab a hold of her coal black hair and begin to pump her face.

But she isn't Puerto Rican anymore. She's a cheerleader. A Mormon cheer-leader. Blonde hair. Full lips. Straight white teeth. Button nose. High boobs.

Tight ass. We're in an empty locker room and she's bent over a bin of soiled linens. I yank down her panties. Push up her skirt. Slide into her from behind. She arches her back and begins to scream. Her ass is small and clean. It slaps against my hips. I grab her pig-tails and pull myself deep inside of her.

Then it's a secretary. A young Jewish secretary. Narrow face. Eyes close together. Classic Jew nose. Brown hair pulled back in a bun. Her breasts are small and perfectly shaped. Her legs are long and slightly knock-kneed. She's sporting a tasteful outfit. Skirt. Matching blazer. High heels. I'm sitting in my office and she's under my desk on her hands and knees. She's sucking my balls while I stroke her face.

She's no longer Jewish. She's Korean. She's a whore. Just like the type my buddies used to bang in the back alley opium dens along the slums of Seoul. But now I'm fucking her. She's 5'1. Ninety-five pounds. Built like a spider monkey. She's on top of me scratching at my chest with long curved nails.

But now it's changing again. Her face is growing older. It's still Korean but wrinkled and haggard and desperate. It's the peasant woman. It's the old peasant woman that I blasted in the face with my M-16 during the massacre at the Changjin reservoir. There's blood and puss pouring from her empty eye and I'm banging her face. I'm jamming my cock into her empty eye socket and I can't stop. And this is how war works. It gets inside you like an infection. It hides in your brain and mingles with your thoughts. It comes out of nowhere and paints all your fantasies black. But I want to bust this nut so I keep banging her bloody face.

Then finally it changes and I'm standing next to a desk in an empty classroom. There's a woman lying on her back on the desk with her dress bunched up around her waist. She isn't wearing any panties and her shaved snatch seems to be winking at me. It's a teacher. A high school teacher. I'm a student. She's asked to see me after class. I lift her legs into the air. Her calves rest on my shoulders. I enter her. She squirms and moans. Her pussy is tight. Almost too tight. Like the hand shake of some pencil-dick cop trying to be a tough guy. I grip her ass with both hands and lift it up off the desk. I feel myself start to climax. I quicken the pace. Her ass makes a rude clapping sound. Faster and faster. Deeper and deeper. We're both screaming and thrashing and then I'm lost in happy thoughts of masculinity and freedom.

I feel it gush out onto my belly. I wipe my hand on my jeans and keep driving. It's all warm and messy. But I don't care. The storm has passed and the sky is blue and my cock is tingling and the Cadillac is purring like a fat lazy farm cat.

I light a Lucky Strike and flip on the radio. I recognize the horn immediately. It's Benny Goodman playing "Happy to Be Here". I turn it up loud and lean back in the seat. Suddenly everything is too cool for school. My past and my future are no longer connected and I'm in the middle someplace where rules no longer matter. I play the steering wheel like a drum set and think about the dead guy and the brief-case and the night which awaits me at the end of the highway.

I arrive in Shreveport at ten o'clock at night. The streets are stark and desperate. I grab a cheap bite at an all-night diner. The waitress has a mustache. The line cook is missing a leg. I find a fly in my coffee. There's a staple in my biscuits and gravy. Some greaser in a hair-net eyes me from the corner booth.

Afterwards I cruise the broken city until I find Emerick Street. It appears as though the town has moved elsewhere. Nothing but shacks and empty warehouses line the dirty street. They're like drunks in a bar at ten past closing. They have nowhere else to go.

A possum scurries across the road. It's the size of a cocker spaniel. I mash on the gas but I miss it. The moon is a whiskey-stained meat-hook. I watch it creep up over the roof tops. Its yellow gaze turns everything stale.

Further up the road I glimpse the Mississippi. It snakes alongside Emerick Street. Silent and dark. I can smell the filthy river as it crawls blindly through the night. The smell is somewhere between moldy hay bails and dead cat-fish.

I see the docks and know I'm getting close. Ancient rickety things perched out over the water. They seem to yearn for the river to rise and put them out of their misery. But the storm never comes and so they waste away like old folks in a retirement home. Ready to die but unable to pull the plug themselves.

With the docks on my right I prowl Emerick Street in search of the drop-off. I start to feel uneasy. The type of unease that comes from doing something you know you shouldn't. Like banging a broad without a condom on. Like sleeping with your best friend's sister. Like rolling a bum for loose change. Like picking a fight with a guy twice your size.

Then I see it. It's a 1938 Ford. It's parked beside the docks. It's glistening in the moon light. As I approach I notice a figure standing beside the car. It's a man. He's the size of an apartment building. He's wearing a fedora and a trench coat. He has a stubby cigar sticking out of his pie-hole. His chest swells and the tip of the stogie glows a cherry red. I coast to a stop in front of the Ford.

When I step out of my Caddy into the bayou darkness I become engulfed in the humidity. The air is thick and oppressive. Insects the size of sparrows chase each other through the Louisiana night.

The man is larger than I had at first thought. He seems to grow with every step I take. When I'm close enough to smell his stale breath I stop. He looms above me like a thunder cloud.

"Can I help you" he mutters from behind his cheap cigar?

"You got it backwards" I say. "It's what I can do for you. I think I got something you might want."

"If that's your idea of a pick-up line you can save it sweet-cheeks. I don't swing that way."

"Don't flatter yourself" I say. "I'm talking for real. I think I got something you might want."

"Somehow I doubt that" he says. "Now beat it. I'm expecting somebody."

"Let me guess" I say. "Old guy. White hair."

"All right kid" he growls. "You win. You got my interest. Now stop playing games and start talking."

"I'm not playing games. I got something for you. Do you want it or not?"

"What is it" he asks?

"I don't have any idea" I say. "It's locked inside a brief-case."

"How the hell did you get it" he asks?

"Last night in Texas some old guy crashed his car. But before he died he asked me to get his briefcase to Shreveport. And here I am."

"Well that's a nice story" he says. "But so is Huckleberry Finn. What do you say we take a look at this briefcase."

"Fuck you very much too" I mumble as I walk toward my car. "Nobody's paying me to do this. I'm just being a nice guy. You could be a little more grateful."

I return with the briefcase and set it down on the dock. I light a smoke and with the light from the match I get a good look at the big man's face. It's a face even a mother would hate. Nose like a hawk's beak. Eyes glazed and bloated. Swollen jowls. And a scar that dances its way down the middle of his face.

"It's all yours" I say.

He bends down to retrieve the case but at the same time reaches in his trench coat and pulls a revolver from a shoulder holster. I'm pissed I didn't see it coming. But now that it's drawn there's nothing I can do. I take a long drag from my Lucky and stare into the hole at the end of the barrel.

"When I mentioned you being more appreciative I was thinking along the lines of a few beers or gas money or a bite to eat maybe."

"Shut the fuck up" he snaps.

"Fair enough."

"You know what I think" he says? "I think you killed him and took the brief-case."

"You know what I think" I respond? "I think you're dumber than a bag of used rubbers. If I had killed him and took his briefcase than why the hell would I come here and risk everything giving it to you?"

I watch his eyes and the instant they veer off in contemplation I strike. I know I will only get one chance so I make it count. I swing at the gun like I'm fixing to decapitate a horse. I knock it loose and it skids across the docks. At the same moment I plant my size eleven in his gonads. He goes cross-eyed and gasps for breath. I run for the gun but he's on top of me. He tackles me onto the dock and it feels like I'm on the bottom of a dog-pile. I stretch for the pistol but it's just beyond my reach and the load in the trench-coat has me pinned. I throw my elbow back in his face. It connects. I feel his nose crack like an egg shell. I squirm loose and grab the gun.

Blood is dripping off the big man's chin when I spin around and face him. He's on his knees with a dazed look on his face. I walk over and stick the barrel against his forehead.

"Start talking you fuck."

"I don't know anything" he says.

"That's fine" I say. "Play dumb. We'll just take a drive down to the police station and tell them what's going on."

"Go ahead" he moans. "Go to the cops. They won't listen to a word you say. They won't even acknowledge your existence."

"All right" I say as I cock the hammer. "I guess we'll try a different approach. How about this one. Start talking or you're a mother fucking grease spot."

"What do you want to know" he asks?

"I want to know why you pulled this gun on me. I want to know who you are. I want to know what's in the God damned briefcase."

"You want to know what I know" he says spitting blood? "Well guess what? I don't know shit. All I know is that everything I thought was real is just a bucket of hog-wash."

"Cut the pig-pen gibberish" I say. "Start making sense."

"I wish I could" he replies.

"Well start by telling me why you pulled the gun on me?"

"Because I was scared" he says. "That's why."

"Scared of what" I ask?

"I don't know" he says. "All I know is that this town is not what it seems. Something ain't right."

"What's in the brief-case" I ask?

"I don't know."

"Quit yanking my chain" I yell. "What's in the fucking brief case?"

"I swear I don't know" he says. "All I know is that it might help explain a few things."

"Well let's open it up and have ourselves a look. What do you say?"

"We can't do that" he says.

"Why not" I ask?

"I don't have the key."

"Who does?"

"It's in a safe place" he says. "A guy I know is keeping an eye on it. You see it's not just me. There's a few of us. I don't call the shots. I was just in charge of picking the thing up."

"Let's keep it simple" I say feeling suddenly very exhausted. "What's your name?"

"Phillip Eckstein."

"Well Phillip" I say eager to find a cheap hotel where I can get some shut-eye. "Stupid as I may be I buy your ignorant act. I'm going to get to the bottom of this but just not right now. It's too fucking late and I've been driving for days on end. We'll get all this taken care of in the morning. You can believe that. And I'm going to hold onto your gun and the briefcase just so you don't get squirrelly. Now tell me where I can find you in the morning."

He gives me the address then crawls inside his 38 Ford. The engine rumbles as he creeps down the street.

"Sorry about the nose job" I shout as I light another smoke and watch the tail-lights disappear into the night.

The moon is now directly overhead. I stare at it and see both scorn and pity in its cold yellow visage. The docks are sad and lonely but for some reason I hang around just listening to the sounds. Maybe I need time for everything to settle in. Maybe I'm looking for conformation that it all actually happened. Maybe I just refuse to admit that I have no place to go and nobody that wants to see me.

I think about the way the gun felt in my hand. Nostalgic and dirty at the same time. Like having sex with an old lover. It felt good but I risk peeling all the scabs off my wounded heart. Lying in a hospital bed with my side bandaged up and my mind doing summersaults in a morphine play-ground I swore I'd never hold a gun again. Bedridden and bloody I wanted nothing more than to sever the chain of violence that had followed me through the years like a stink I could never wash off. But here I am sucking a Lucky in Shreveport in the early morning with a .357 tucked in the small of my back.

Maybe I just need to accept my lot. I can change my nature no more than I can rinse the black from my hair or scrub the blue from my eyes. Everybody has a knack for something. I have one for violence. I don't like it. I'm not proud of it. I've just always been good at it. From school yard quarrels to parking lot show-downs. From bare-knuckled matches in smoke-filled warehouses to gun battles in the mountains. Whatever the scene the outcome is the same. But where is this path leading? To a life of emptiness and pain? To a shallow grave along some highway in the middle of nowhere? To hell and beyond?

I find a travel lodge on the outskirts of town. It's a beat little dive with a dusty parking lot and a broken ice machine. The inbred working the front office has a harelip and three teeth. Tobacco spit stains the front of his overalls. His left eye is lazy while the right eye tries to compensate. It's too awake. Too alert. It seems to stare into my business and invade my privacy.

My room has a squeaky bed. A cracked mirror. A busted clock. An ancient radio. I put the brief-case in the dresser and slip the .357 under the pillow. I find a jazz station and crawl into bed. The vacancy sign flashes its red neon through my curtains. It lights up my room like some bawdry Vegas whore-house. I slip my hand under the pillow and grip the Smith and Wesson. I close my eyes and drift off to the sound of a bass and a trumpet and a snare drum.

My sleep is packed with twisted dreams. Dreams of violence and sex and perversity. In one dream I'm back in Korea fighting in the war. But I'm not fighting Koreans. I'm fighting an army of briefcases. The briefcases are full of dismembered bodies. Severed heads. Twisted legs. Broken arms. Bones and entrails. Every time I kill a briefcase it cracks open and dumps its sloppy load onto the dirt like a miscarriage. The body parts begin to slither toward one another. They connect. They fit together like a hideous puzzle. It's turning into me. I watch in horror as my head rolls up my body and perches itself on my bloody shoulders. The more briefcases I kill the more of me there are. Eventually there is an entire horde of hodge-podge corpses. They form a single file line. It stretches into the horizon. At the front of the line is a bamboo hut. The corpses are entering through the door one at a time. I run to the window and peer in. There is my ex-girlfriend Susan. She's lying on a pile of hay with her legs cracked open like a greasy wish-bone. One after the other they spread her knees and have their way. Corpse after corpse until Susan like a thanksgiving turkey can hold no more and seeps the stuffing of rancid jizz onto her throne of hay and mud. I barge in the hut and cut to the front of the line. I drop my drawers and take my turn but the pussy is so big and broken that I just fall in. I tumble blindly through her tunnel of whoredom. I land in something soft and pink. But to my surprise it isn't the bottom of her cunt. It's a blanket. A pink blanket. My baby blanket. I'm wrapped up in it. Snuggled inside my crib. And there is my mother standing above me. She's dressed in marine corps fatigues. She's holding a baby bottle shaped like a dildo and she's shouting at me in Korean. She screams and screams but I don't understand a word. When I fail to respond she starts stabbing me in the eye with the rubber dick. And there I die by the hands of my dead mother in a pool of cadaver cum at the bottom of my ex-girlfriends stretched-out cunt while behind me an army of briefcase entrails wait for sloppy seconds.

▼

CHAPTER 3

A HANDLE AS SEXY AS THE DAME WHO HOLDS IT

I hear the highway growling outside my window like the stomach of a starving vagrant. Sunlight is hitting me in the face through the crack in the curtains. The gun is still in my hand. The radio is still on. I stare up at the ceiling and feel as though I could be anyone. Just another nameless tramp in a soulless motel. The outcome of my own nations misguided evolution. The final product of a soul-sucking song and dance called middle America. Billy Holliday comes on the radio. I turn it up loud then jump in the shower and get dressed.

Outside in the morning sun my Cadillac glimmers like a perverse inclination. I throw the briefcase in the trunk and lay tracks in search of a hole in the wall diner where I can get a cheap bite and some coffee.

I find a restaurant in the slums. It's wedged between a wig shop and a laundry mat. Its windows are dark and streaked with grease. I push open the door. A bell rings. Nobody looks my way. Everyone remains hunched over their plates. Heads bowed in praise of their own omnipotent tragedies.

I park myself in a booth at the back of the joint and give a nod to the young tail peddling the slop. She hurries over with a menu and a cup of coffee. Her name tag reads Tiffany. She isn't the sharpest looking stick in the bunch. Ratty hair. A chipped tooth. A glaze in her eyes. Hers appears to be the brand of stupidity that is acquired over time. Received not through birth but from a vicious blow to the head at some point in her childhood. Did she fall in a well? Did she get kicked in the face by a horse? Did she get ran over by a tractor? Or did a high school boyfriend get too drunk one night and crack her upside the skull with a two-by-four? But despite her cock-eyed appearance she's a skillful waitress. Regular in one hand. Decaf in the other. She twirls around the deadbeat diner like an inbred marionette.

After a fat stack of flap-jacks and enough coffee to hospitalize an old woman I drop some bread on the table and hit the streets to find Mr. Eckstein.

The town looks different with caffeine in my system. My eyes are stretched wide and hungry for all the details. The streets are all crooked and twisted. Backwards avenues leading the dumb and blind on a pilgrimage to the outskirts of wherever.

A busted hydrant tosses its ghetto jizz into the stale air. Black boys in broken sneakers chase a three legged dog down a red brick alley. Tiny-bopper dames in pink bobby socks clutch books to their chests and skip down the sidewalk toward some beat-up junior high. Enigmatic strangers with jack-o-lantern eyes and hallow secrets crawl across the town like ants on a cat carcass. A raggedy hobo with a paper bag of cheap liquor is tossing a piss in the middle of a deserted switching yard. A couple of teenage greasers with tight shirts and rolled-up jeans stand at a bus stop sharing a smoke. Two chubby coppers sit in a black-and-white eating doughnuts waiting for a knuckle-head motorist to race by. An old man in overalls sucking a corncob pipe stands on the pier dangling a fishing line in the muddy Mississippi.

The town is a tapestry of freak-shows and oddballs. A hodge-podge of all that is grotesque. A testament to all that is southern and American.

Eckstein's place is a dumpy loft apartment above a gas station downtown. I park my Caddy in the back alley. There are wooden stairs leading up to his door. I tuck the piece in my belt. The steel feels cold against the small of my back.

I dart up the stairs and give his door a good rapping. No answer. I knock again. No answer. I have a hunch Eckstein got a case of the chicken shits and split town or is inside hiding like a rat.

"Rise and shine" I holler as I knock again on the door.

Still no answer. So I pound. The door creaks open slowly. I stick my head in and take a look around. The joint is a wreck. It stinks like the snatch of a Harlem whore after a weekend of two-for-one specials. I close the door behind me and cut through the kitchen. Cockroaches scatter across the cheap linoleum. The counter top is all dirty dishes and fruit flies. When I see the living-room I know something is wrong. There's debris scattered everywhere. Furniture has been knocked over. The place has been ransacked. I draw the piece and cut across the living-room and down the hallway. I come to a door on my right. I take a deep breath then kick the mother wide open.

There is a bed. Eckstein is laying on it. Dead. Spread eagle. He looks like a kid making snow angels in the play-ground field. His limbs are stretched apart. His lifeless eyes wide open. He's been shot in the face with a high caliber weapon. The hole in his forehead is the size of a quarter. Blood and brain bits dribble from his face. The sheets are all soaked red.

My legs go weak. My stomach jumps up in my throat. I stick my hand over my mouth to stifle the urge to spew vomit. I spin around and belligerently stagger down the hallway.

When I reach the door I lunge outside and suck in the fresh air wildly. With each gulp I feel my composure return. My thoughts become manageable. The feeling of nausea passes.

I glance down at the parking lot. That's when I see it. My car. Some cock sucker has pried open my trunk. The briefcase is gone.

I'm instantly down the stairs. Pistol pointed. Heart racing. Some sneaky prick has been keeping an eye on me. I'm pissed. I throw my wide-eyed rage gaze all over looking for the fucker that's jacked the briefcase. In the bushes. Up the trees. Down the alleys. Behind the cars. The windows. The doorways. The nooks. The crannies.

Nothing. Nobody. Whoever it was isn't sticking around to exchange pleasantries. They were fast. Slippery. In and out. Case closed. I stick the gun in my belt and slam the trunk shut then pound on the roof of the Caddy.

Across the street is a five story apartment building. All dirty brick and bent metal. Pigeons cling to the rusty fire escapes. They coo and tremble and drop their runny white crap onto the sad heads of shmuck pedestrians. Broken windows. Torn curtains. Crumbling eaves. Trash cans in the alley below spilling their rotten filth onto the oily pavement. Tomcats with infected eyes hiss and scratch and fight over fish bones and rusty old cans of beans.

I assume the building's occupants are all crippled dead-beats with poisoned souls. Middle-aged whores with gashes the size of the Mississippi too saggy and worn to make ends meet but too dumb from decades of abuse to land a legit job. Junky skeletons with yellow eyes and loose teeth sitting in musty chairs with cigarette burns jamming dirty needles into their scabby arms. A starving artist with a skull full of reefer and a heart full of poetic revolution sitting in front of a clunky type writer while crackling bebop pours from an ancient record player. A war vet back in the states with nothing to do but drink himself to death in a lonely nightmare tenement. A welfare mom pissed at the world and screaming at her unwanted children.

Then as if to rebuke my assumptions I see her in the upstairs window. A thing of rare beauty. A vision. A longing. A dirty dream. There is a lot of hair. This I can see. Light brown and lovely with streaks of blonde. Long. Flowing. Curling. Sexy. Natural. There is something intense about the size of her hair. Something vibrant and alive. Free and savage. The type of hair that I want to thrust my hands into while having sex. Hair that I can tug and yank. And that face. Man-o-live that face. Desperate. Needy. Hungry. Seductive. Sassy. Perfect. It is somehow dominant and timid at the same time. Her face reminds me of the first time I masturbated.

It comes as a big surprise to see a foxy dame in such a beat joint. At first I just stare. Tongue hanging out. Knees weak. Dick pulsating in my Levis. With her beauty comes forgetfulness. What briefcase? What dead body? What rage? All I know is that with just one look she has captivated me like no other.

But then it hits me. She might have seen something. I'm suddenly sucked back into the moment. Filled again with rage and trembling anxiety. I bolt across the street. Horns honking. Tires squealing. Darting in and out of traffic like a frightened dog. When she sees me running she backs away from the window and lets the curtains fall into place.

"Hey wait" I yell waving my arms and jumping up and down on the sidewalk. "Hey Miss. Did you see anything? Hey lady. Did you see anybody messing with my car? Hello. Anybody up there?"

I yell for a full minute. Jumping around like some high school cheerleader. Nothing. No response. I give up and head back across the street when I hear something above me. I look up just in time to see her slender white arms pulling the window closed. There is a piece of paper. Slightly crumbled. Falling through the air. Spiraling downwards like a little bird with a busted wing. I grab it out of the air. Curious. Excited.

It reads "THE BLUE ROOM AT TEN 'O CLOCK."

I look up again but she's gone. Just the decaying building looming above me with its shiny dead windows. The pale sky. The lazy clouds. The oppressive idea of infinite space.

I jump in my Cadillac and hit the road. It feels as though my face is going to break. My thoughts are too big. Too many who's. Too many why's.

I watch the city flow by like a silent film. The buildings are old and filled with secrets. The cracks in the sidewalks are sinister smiles. The traffic signs are symbolic messages. The world is an enigmatic hemorrhoid on the asshole of infinity. All is chaos.

But as I drive I realize my confusion is dependant upon one question. Do I want to follow this thing through to the end or get the fuck out of Dodge? The answer becomes apparent through my actions. I'm driving fast. But I'm not going anywhere. I keep making circles. I'm not leaving Shreveport. As much as I want to I can't. How can I? A seedy town. A dead body. A missing briefcase. A foxy dame. It's just starting to get good.

So I decide that I won't leave Shreveport until I find the briefcase. Until I discover what's inside. Until I figure out what's going on. It isn't the brightest decision I've ever made. But bright was never my bag of meat.

I hunt down a cheap flop where I can crash. The dive is beat. Downtown. Dirty bricks. Small room on the top floor of a crumby hotel. Twelve by twelve with a piss-stained mattress and a banged up radio and a window overlooking the poverty. Across the street is a rundown cinema. Its bright red neon burns like a great false hope.

It is to be my home for a while. I accept it with patience and understanding. Like a mother with a retarded child. I turn on the radio and find a good jazz station. I lock the door and kick off my shoes. I stick my piece under the pillow and settle in for a nap.

I crash hard. Out cold. Dreams of a sordid variety. Tangled images of trash and violence. Demented housewives and dirty truckers. Bloody hammers and broken pitchforks. Crippled children with perverted pacifiers. Fist fights and chicken coups. Pig-pens and barnyards. Tractors and shotguns. Whiskey and cow shit. Pain and understanding. Tits and ass. Switchblades and horsepower.

I wake up soaked in sweat. On the verge of screaming. It's late. The room is dark. I hit the lights and check my watch. It's nine-thirty. I'm almost late. I crank up the radio and start pulling myself together.

The Blue Room is a swanky joint. I can smell the decadence as I approach. The muscle-bound monkey working the door eyes me like a bum because my get-up didn't set me back two bills. I stare him down until his tough guy demeanor cracks like a child's skull. He steps aside and lets me in.

The interior is a claustrophobic's nightmare. Too many tables. Too many employees. Too many pretentious patrons with old money drinking top notch liquor. It's dimly lit. The smoke is suffocating. I make my way through the crowded bar and take a seat by the empty stage. I recline in my chair and scan the room for the mystery woman.

A waiter approaches. He's dainty. He has perfect teeth and slicked hair and a sharp mustache. He smiles big. It's all show. I order a dry martini and tell him to step on it. He returns promptly. I pour the beverage down my throat and order another one.

I'm nursing my fourth martini when the room goes black. A light shines on center stage. The curtains pull apart. The house goes crazy. The show is starting. I bite into my gin-soaked olive and eye the stage restlessly.

The first thing I see is the hair. Same as before. Vibrant. Alive. I sit up in my chair with my eyes as big as pie pans. Her body has more curves than the Pacific Coast Highway. She's wearing a sleek black dress. It covers her like a coat of fresh paint. There's a slit that runs up to her hip. Her cleavage is prominent and ample. She moves into the light. Center stage. The crowd falls silent. Mesmerized. Behind her the band kicks in. She grips the microphone and begins to sing. It's a slow jazz number. "Lights Out" by Ella Fitzgerald. Her voice is husky and thick but entirely feminine. Her body sways seductively. I watch her with wonder. Feeling as though I've slipped into a lucid wet dream.

The set consists of seven or eight standards. After the last song the performers disappear behind the closing curtains. Suddenly she's at my table.

"Anyone sitting here?"

"Yes" I reply. "You are."

She takes a seat. Orders a cocktail.

"After this mornings disappearing act I never would of guessed you to be such an exhibitionist."

"A girl has to be careful where she performs."

"Why's that" I ask?

"Not every audience is a safe one" she says.

"Go on."

"There's some shady people around town."

"I'm listening."

"I don't even know what I'm talking about" she says suddenly getting cold feet. "I shouldn't have asked you here. I've said too much already."

"What are you talking about? You haven't said anything. What's going on around here? Something's not right with this town and I got a feeling you know something."

"Slow down" she says. "There is something going on in this town and that's exactly why I'm hesitant to talk to you. I don't even know who you are."

"What do you want to know" I ask?

"I want to know I can trust you" she says. "That's all. Tell me who you are and I'll tell you what I know."

"Well" I say. "My full name is Buckley Finch Wilder."

"And" she asks?

"I'm twenty-seven."

"I mean who you really are" she says. "Tell me something interesting. Something private."

"I'm the type of prick that will stick my thumb in your ass without telling you first."

"Now you're getting it" she says.

"I leave the lights on when I'm having sex. I prefer to eat by myself. I don't like sharing."

"Good" she says.

"I like dressing sharp and taking long walks through the city at night where I can meet strangers and talk about jazz and god and poetry and firearms. I once put the moves on my aunt's best-friend."

"Excellent" she says. "Go on."

"I once kicked my best-friend's ass because he double-dog-dared me I wouldn't. I like smoking marijuana and then falling asleep in the bathtub listening to Duke Ellington and eating doughnuts."

"Yes" she exclaims.

"I like walking out of bars at ten-thirty in the morning with my shades on and knowing the joke is on everyone else. I once took a crowbar to a fist-fight. I like listening to Bing Crosby albums and drinking eggnog and thinking about my childhood Christmases in L.A. when my mom and dad were still alive."

"OK" she says. "That's enough."

"Well" I ask?

"Well I don't know if I like you" she says. "But I have a feeling I can trust you."

"Thanks doll-face but it takes two to teeter-totter. It's your turn to spill the beans."

She leans in over the table. Close. Intimate. I can smell the vodka on her breath. I can see the loneliness in her eyes.

"It could be nothing" she says. "I don't know. All I know is that there are some people around town who've been acting awfully strange."

"What about my car" I ask? "Did you see something this morning?"

"I saw the trunk pop open" she says. "And something came out of it. That's it."

"You didn't see anybody take a briefcase?"

"No" she says. "Why? What was in the briefcase?"

"I don't know. But I have a hunch it's got something to do with what's going on around town. Now is there anything else you know that might help me? Anything at all?"

"I've heard talk of an old man who lives outside of town" she says. "His name's Jarvis Beauchamp. People say he's crazy. But I've also heard he might know something about what's going on."

"Why did you drop that note to me this morning" I ask? "Why did you tell me this stuff?"

"I don't know" she says. "It just seemed like you needed some help. Plus I was bored and you looked kind of interesting."

She tosses back her cocktail and stands up to split.

"Hey wait" I call out. "I didn't even get your name."

"Read it on your way out" she says with a wink. "It's written in big red letters on the marquee out front."

Her name is Veronica Vaughn. A handle as sexy as the dame who holds it. It's become lodged in my mind. Like a fox-tail in a dog's paw. I repeat it endlessly. I like the way it rolls off my lips. Even later at night as I lie in the darkness of my two-bit shit-hole I continue to whisper it. It conjures images of hair and boobs and legs and jazz. I can't stop. The more I say it the clearer her image becomes. Standing on the stage with that phallic microphone pressed close to her hungry mouth. Her legs going all the way up.

My cock gets hard as a rock and I know it will be a long night unless I put it to rest. So I let my mind wander. My hand becomes her mouth. My fingers are her lips. She kisses down my chest. She licks across my belly. She engulfs my manhood. Gentle. Sweet. Efficient. She yearns for it. She needs it. She works it. Deeper. Faster. Harder.

It doesn't take long. My orgasm arrives with the magnitude of a barrel full of buckshot. It spurts into the air like a party favor and lands on my belly. But like most good highs it splits as quick as it shows up and I'm left soiled and unsatisfied.

I stare out the window into the neon night. I feel vulnerable and alone. I'm in over my head. Something foul is at play. I feel the fear fall upon me. A cold intangible doom. Not knowing what else to do I begin smearing the cum across my belly and chest. I want to wear it like a shield. A suit of armor. A security blanket. I rub it over my entire body. My arms. My legs. My face. It's familiar. It's safe. I spark a Lucky and under the soft glow of the cigarette my body glistens like a new born baby.

My world is being torn in two. Ripped at the seams like small pants on a fat ass. No connection to my past. No certainty of my future. I reside somewhere between these two extremes. Groveling through the darkness like a blind rat. Searching for that definitive moment of clarity and truth. But I know I will find it. I'm not alone. I have my .357 and my knuckles and my semen to protect me.

CHAPTER 4

▼

A FIFTH OF CUTTY SARK AND A FRESH PACK OF LUCKY'S

I wake-up naked and disoriented. Hung-over. Sweaty. Tangled up in my sheets like a hog-tied tom-cat. My body as unfamiliar as the surrounding walls. That's when it hits me. A haunting conclusion. Life is like a poorly directed film. Damn thing's half over and you still don't know what the hell's going on. But I've never been able to walk out of a movie. I'm a cheap son of a bitch and I like to get my moneys worth.

So I shoot out of bed lickety-split. Ready to start the day. Ready to make sense out of this low budget picture show. I crank out a hundred push-ups and a hundred sit-ups then hit the john at the end of the hall. Shit. Shower. Shave. I toss on some fresh threads and start searching for a fellow named Jarvis Beauchamp.

After a quick look in the phonebook yields zero leads I hit the streets. Downtown is thick with society's dregs. A perfect place to start my hunt. Gutters and alleys. Dives and diners. Parks and bus-stops. Bars and bowling alleys. Pool-halls and arcades. The steam and the stench. The cigarette smoke and the bacon fat.

I mingle. I schmooze. I bull-shit. I rub elbows with the transient souls of Shreveport. God's lost children. Shysters and bums. Hustlers and grease-bags. Drunks and dopers. Sluts and skanks. Hobos and angels.

I bump into a wino on the corner of someplace and wherever. Rotten skin. Dead teeth. Empty eyes. Breath like a suitcase full of road-kill. I ask if he knows Jarvis Beauchamp and he says he'll squeal for a jug of booze. I play along and grab him a pint of Jim Beam. He takes a deep pull then starts talking. He says Jarvis is a cross-eyed Cherokee who used to play horse shoes with Satan on top of the empire state building. He tells me he and Jarvis once drank an ocean of monkey's blood then fucked each other in the back of an invisible box-car. He brags of the time he and Jarvis barbequed fifteen midgets and mashed their meat into patties that they sold at the circus in the year 1397. It doesn't take a psychology degree to realize this fellow is two broads short of an orgy. But I feel sorry for him. I let him keep the bottle. Maybe the sauce is his only means of salvation.

I give up in the early afternoon and hunker down in a Ma and Pa deli with a reuben and a tall vanilla malt. It's here I find the tip I'm looking for. Two hill-billy farm boys are sitting in the booth behind me. They smell like sheep shit and look like Step and Fetch-it gone inbred.

"Do I pick my nose too much" I hear one ask.

"Does Mama fart when she eats chili?"

"Shit yea she does."

"Well there you have it."

"But I don't really think it's picking my nose because I only use my thumb and pinky."

"Doesn't matter if you use a shovel or a shoe-horn. If you're pulling boogers out of your face you're picking your nose."

"Maybe you're right."

"Damn right I'm right."

"But Pappy picks his nose more than I do. I'm going to tell him you think he picks his nose too much."

"You do and I'll split your face for you. Besides Pappy don't count. He puts a hanky around his finger. So that isn't picking."

"Horse shit it isn't picking. He goes wrist deep. You could put a rubber on your finger but picking's picking."

"You're ignorant is all. Don't have no manners."

"Yea well you dress funny."

"Well your Mama's fatter than a ten pound tic."

"You shit for brains. We're brothers. You're making fun of your own damn Mama."

"Who's making fun? She's fat isn't she?"

"Yea. She's fat."

"Well there you go dip-stick."

"I got your dip-stick shit-face."

Try as I might I can't block out their barnyard banter. Like listening to some inane comedy show on a radio with a busted volume. I scope the cleavage on the broad behind the counter. Gawk at the middle-aged tail pouring coffee. Dig my greasy reuben. Read the paper. Eye the cherry rides rolling slow along the street. Nothing works. Their words are an itch that is immune to scratching. I just can't ignore them.

"Did you hear Aunt Matilda got that tumor removed?"

"No I didn't. I don't care to either."

"Fucking thing weighed forty-seven pounds."

"You got manure in your ears? I said I don't want to hear about it. How am I going to eat my grits with you flapping your lips about a forty-seven pound tumor?"

"Sorry. I didn't know you were eating."

"The hell you reckon I'm doing over here? Shitting in reverse?"

"Quite your fussing. I said I'm sorry."

"Sorry shmorry. You're always talking about grody shit when it's not called for. Like that time I brought Miss Darlene to the house on a date and you had to show us all them dead mice you kept in that empty whiskey bottle. And you had to ramble on about that pregnant one that was so fat she barely fit in the bottle. And about how your thumb got all slimy and gooey from trying to shove it in there. You and that filthy mouth of yours went and ruined my date."

"It's not like you would of gotten laid anyhow looser."

"Look who's talking. You haven't seen pussy in so long you'd probably try to kill it with a sling-shot."

"Like you're any better. Only chance you have of getting inside a woman is visiting the statue of liberty. But that's not going to happen because you're afraid to leave Mama."

"You know what?"

"What?"

"I used to hate you real good. Used to think you were about as useful at tits on bacon. But now I just feel sorry for you. I think you've finally lost it."

"Lost what?"

"Exactly. You know who you're starting to remind me of? You remind me of old man Beauchamp. That's right. You're as crazy as old man Beauchamp."

The name slaps me across the face like the hand of a jealous dame. I scarf the last bite of reuben and turn around.

"Are you guys referring to Jarvis Beauchamp" I ask?

"Maybe we are and maybe we're not" says the bigger of the two. "Who wants to know?"

"Mr. none of your business. That's who. And if I want to play games I'll go buy a deck of cards. So if either of you know something start singing."

"Give me one good reason."

"I'll give you two good reasons mother fucker" and I hold up both my fists.

"There's two of us and only of you."

"Does it look like I care" I ask? "Now I'm giving you one last chance. Start yapping or you'll be drinking your food through a straw for the rest of your miserable days."

We play the staring game far an eternity. Nobody says a word. Nobody moves a muscle. In their eyes I see both fear and curiosity. Like two young boys who can't decide whether to pet the stray dog with the matted fur and the crazy eyes. In the end they prove good judges of character. They decide not to test the validity of my threats.

"Yea" says the big one. "We're talking about Jarvis Beauchamp. Why do you ask?"

"Because I want to meet him that's why. Now where can I find him?"

"He owns the land next to our Pappy's farm. About twenty miles north of town. 1201 Sugar Creek Road. But what do you want with him for? He's crazier than a shit house rat."

"That's my favorite type" I say as I drop some cash and head for the door.

So I take a nice long drive. The late summer sun is a cheap bawdry red. It's the color of a prostitute's lipstick. The air is thick and fertile. Smells like heavy sex in a small room. I pass a drive-in on the outskirts of town. It reminds me of the first time I felt a girl's breasts. It was Pasadena 1940. Starlight Theatre. Some Bogart gangster flick. Two sleeping bags. A flat-bed Ford. A flask of Old Crow. Heavy petting. Dry humping. A hard-on like a railroad nail. The God damned bra strap finally coming undone. Pink skin as smooth as glass. That explosive first orgasm that filled my drawers with a gallon of mess. All was Hollywood glamour. All was childhood fantasy. All was hot-rods and hand-jobs. All was fun in the sun and red white and blue.

Now I'm in the country. Trees instead of buildings. Pastures instead of parks. Cows instead of pedestrians. My Caddy leaves a wake of dust a mile long. White walls spinning. Big Jay McNeely blaring from the speakers. Lucky Strike smoke billowing out the window. I feel a rush of excitement. That fleeting joy that only comes when the music is pumping and you're doing eighty plus behind the wheel of a huge American machine.

I hit Sugar Creek Road. The address is not hard to find. A tremendous wrought iron archway stands over the gravel driveway. The number 1201 is positioned boldly on top. I cut a hard right. The driveway is a mile long and crooked as a busted nose. It's lined with oak trees. Massive growths holding hands above the road.

When I reach the end of the drive I'm confronted by a mansion of spectacular size. One of those fabulous homes that can only exist in the deep south. Turn around drive with a fountain in the middle. Classic architecture. Columns stretching from porch to gable. The whole thing white with barn-red trim.

I kill the tunes and coast to a stop. Get out of my car and take the steps two at a time. Double doors a mile high. Solid. Stately. I give them a good knocking. Almost immediately they swing wide open. Standing inside is a black woman.

She's as old as the trees that line the drive. She stands bent slightly at the hip. Her attire alludes to the role of maid or caregiver. Her hands are withered little things. The veins disturbingly large. Her face is severe but not unkind. Skin as black as the jungle at night. Eyes penetrating and bottomless. Teeth big and white and long.

"Can I help you sir" she asks with a voice conditioned by years of servitude?

"I was told that a man by the name of Jarvis Beauchamp lives here."

"Yes sir. This is his home. May I ask what your business is with Mr. Beauchamp?"

"It's private. I would prefer to speak only with him."

"Sir" she says. "I handle all of Mr. Beauchamp's affairs."

"I understand. But this is very important and I would prefer to talk to Mr. Beauchamp."

"I'm afraid that's impossible sir" she says. "Are you not aware of Mr. Beauchamp's condition?"

"No. I'm not. But I need to see him. Please. Just for a minute."

"I'm going to allow you to see him" she says glancing over her shoulders as though nervous of bending the rules. "But I need you to understand that he's not well. He's a fragile man. I ask that you treat him so. I'm giving you five minutes."

"It's a deal" I say.

She leads me up a long winding flight of stairs. We reach the second story hallway and turn left. The house is clean. Too clean. Perfect. Immaculate. Sterile. It doesn't feel like a home. More like a hospital. A sanitarium. A place where people go to drool and urinate and stretch their minds like chewing gum. There's a door at the end of the hallway. It's closed. She knocks softly.

"Mr. Beauchamp" she whispers as she pushes open the door. "There's a gentleman here to see you."

I see Jarvis Beauchamp crouched on the floor beside the window. He's wearing blue pajamas. He's clutching his knees to his chest like a hundred and fifty pound fetus. The evening sun falls harshly upon his face. It's anything but flattering. His ancient skin appears gray and fragile. His hair is thick. Unruly. An unhealthy yellow. Color of nicotine-stained fingers. Withered lips. Deep wrinkles. Big nose. Hairy ears.

I approach but my presence elicits no response. He isn't frightened. He isn't excited. I'm not sure he's even aware. He just sits there on the floor. Clutching himself and staring out the window.

There's a peculiar look in his sunken eyes. It appears as though he's contemplating some immense and all-important concept. I have a hunch he's been contemplating it for a very long time.

"The name's Buckley Wilder" I say as I hunker down beside him. "The old lady that runs this show is only giving me five minutes so I'll keep this short. The rumor I heard is that you think something's wrong with this town. That there's something going on. I want to know what it's all about. I want to know what you know."

He turns and faces me. His eyes have lost their stupid glaze. They're now sharp as pitch-forks. Piercing. Deranged. Enlightened.

"Who would be born must first destroy a world" he says. "The bird flies to God."

I'm stunned. His words are beautiful. But despite their beauty they make no more sense than a two legged pony. I press on.

"I don't understand" I say. "What is it you're trying to say?"

"Who would be born must first destroy a world. The bird flies to God."

"Mr. Beauchamp I don't get it. You need to help me understand. This is important. Someone has been killed. You need to tell me what's going on."

He speaks again but only repeats the same statement.

"Listen" I say. "Cut the fucking riddles. This has to do with me. With who I am. I need to know the truth. Give it to me straight."

He pushes me out of the way and jumps onto the bed. I've pressed too hard. His delicate mind has finally popped like a cherry. It's painful to watch. His decrepit old body struggling to meet the demands of his hay-wire mind. Banging his fists. Tearing apart pillows. Spit flying from his lips. Screaming out his mani-acal mantra over and over again.

I slip out of the room. I can't take it anymore. It's sad to see a mind that far gone. Like seeing a once-boss rig rusting in the junkyard. I'm walking down the stairs shaking my head when the caretaker stops me.

"You shouldn't pity him" she says. "He's not crazy."

"Of course not" I say as I continue down the stairs. "He's as sharp as a God damned switch-blade."

"It's not as simple as you think" she says. "He wasn't always like this. It started years ago. This is just the unfortunate end. He's still in there though. And he still has a lot of ideas in that head of his. Unfortunately he lacks the means to express them."

"What happened to him" I ask?

"It's very strange" she says. "Very strange indeed. Even the doctors can't explain it. It has to do with Mr. Beauchamp's love of literature. As a child he could never be seen without a book in his hands. It was the same when he was an adult. Which is when I came into his service. He was bright. Charismatic. He flourished as a businessman in his early years. But his true love was always books. So much so that he would memorize lines. Quotes. Passages. He had a line for every occasion. His memory was amazing. It got to the point when he simply ceased to speak for himself. He communicated only through the words of his favorite authors. This was odd but it was no cause for alarm. He still functioned well with society. The problem arose when the first of his favorite writers died. I believe it was Mark Twain. When he died Mr. Beauchamp lost the ability to draw upon his words. It was tragic. And over the years as more writers died his ability to communicate became less and less. For a while we had hope because he found new writers to quote. But even that has recently stopped. One by one they've died and he's left with next to nothing. He loved the work of Thomas Wolfe and James Joyce. When they died he was reduced to barely anything at all. And now you've seen what he has become."

"How many authors are still alive" I ask?

"Only one remains" she says. "It sounds cruel but sometimes I wish that writer would die so that Jarvis could be silent. Peaceful. Dignified."

"Who's the writer" I ask?

"The words he speaks are from a book entitled Demian" she says. "Are you familiar with the German author Herman Hesse?"

"I've heard of him but I haven't read his work" I answer.

"Well" she says. "That is what Mr. Beauchamp has been reduced to. One writer. One quote. One fate. Peculiar isn't it?"

"Fucking-A" I say as I proceed down the stairs and out the door. "Fucking-A."

On my way back to Shreveport I spot someone tailing me. The bastard pulls onto the road right behind me about ten miles north of town. He isn't hard to spot. He follows me with the subtlety of a ten year old boy chasing the ice cream man down the middle of the road a on a hot summer day. I mash the gas. My Caddy slices through the twilight but I can't ditch those menacing headlights. Then a thought cracks my noggin like a Joe Louis hook. Am I getting tailed? Or am I getting whacked? I don't plan on finding out. I jam it into high gear and rip across the dusk-stained countryside.

When I reach the outskirts of town the son of a bitch is closer than ever. But I know if I can make it downtown I can give him the slips. I push my Caddy full throttle. Gunning for the heart of Shreveport. Weaving in and out. Cutting right. Jerking left. Screaming like a banshee. Mother fucker stays right on my ass.

I bolt down Main Street. The city is bright and alive. Cars cruising. People smoking and laughing. Movies and music. Vendors and bums. I see it all and it's all a blur. Melting into one long electric smear. A neon smudge called civilization. I tear through the middle of it. Barreling. Oblivious. Determined. Running reds. Whipping U-turns. Shooting down the alleys. But my plan isn't working for shit. He's still right behind me.

I know what I have to do. I have to stop playing his game. I take Main to Front Street then open her up. One hundred yards up Front Street I check my rearview and see him come skidding around the corner. I crank the wheel and tug the emergency brake. The car whips a perfect one-eighty. Tires screeching like some nagging housewife. I punch the clutch and send a cloud of burning rubber into the air. The tires catch the road and off I roar to meet my pursuer head on.

Chicken is a game I know well. You have to be willing to win or die. And I am. I spent many summer nights growing up in southern Cal taking pink slips from blow-hards who let their alligator mouths run off with their hummingbird asses.

So I race towards him. My Caddy getting rubber in all four gears. His car building speed. I can tell by his headlights he's driving a Chevy. Not that it matters. Chevy. Ford. Studebaker. I don't give a shit if he's ridding horse-back. Either he pulls over or we both go up in a ball of burning metal. I curl my lip in a vicious sneer and aim right at him. Forty yards. Thirty yards. Twenty yards. I see flashes of mayhem. Death in all its unflattering guises. Gun battles. Head locks. Flame throwers. Piles of dead Koreans. The face of oblivion stretching its vortex mouth to swallow my bones and suck the marrow from my soul. Ten yards. Five yards.

He cuts to his right and crashes into a dumpster. Just another chump who played pussy-get-fucked with the wrong son of a bitch. I speed off into the night. Howling like some alpha male challenging the pack.

I'm left a bit shook up though. My nerves are shot. I need something to take the edge off. I swing by a liquor store and spring for a fifth of Cutty Sark and a fresh pack of Lucky's. I cruise the beat streets for a place to be alone with my thoughts and my vices. I find an embankment beside the base of a bridge downtown. I park my rig and kill the engine. I crank on the jazz station and sit on the hood with my booze and my smokes.

I think about the jam I'm in. About the events that transpired to leave me in the here and the now. The crash on the highway in Texas. The drop-off on the docks gone terribly awry. Eckstein catching a hole in the head. The note falling from the sky like a crippled angel. The conversation with Veronica Vaughn. The two farm boys jaw-jabbering in the booth behind me. The meeting with Jarvis Beauchamp. The game of chicken I was just forced to play. It all seems like an absurd riddle. An elaborate code that requires deciphering if I'm to move forward on my quest for the truth.

Mr. Beauchamp has more than a few screws loose but I still believe he's a piece to the puzzle. His words are insane but also prophetic. What had he meant? What truth was he trying to convey? These questions leave me feeling as though my head is a piece of chicken gristle stuck between the teeth of a syphilis-ridden clown.

I swig good and deep from the bottle. The alcohol is having a melancholy effect on my soul. A Benny Goodman tune is on the radio and it meshes with the sounds of the city to create a melody that's sadder than either one alone. I take another pull of whiskey then light a smoke.

Shreveport dances below me with an impoverished grace. The soft mindless ebb and flow of humanity. The hideous parade of America at night. The endless saga of concrete and flesh. The sweaty shuffle of weary souls. The city is an electric face. It winks its pompous neon eyes. As if to gloat. As if to spurn. As if to rub it in that I'm not needed for it to exist.

I feel so disconnected. So lonely. I want only to belong but it seems as though every step I take only distances me further from the bonds of mankind. I want to shed my skin of self-reliance and wander the earth naked. Humble. Meek.

The booze is hitting me hard. My loneliness continues to fester. I take a long drag off my Lucky and lean back on the hood. Something about the stars and the jazz makes me think of Veronica Vaughn. I think about the way she moved across the stage. Her body hotter than a Missouri barn with a sheet metal roof in the middle of summer. But there's something else. It has to do with her kind eyes. Her sultry demeanor. There's a duality in her that entices me. She strikes me as the type of dame who would take you to the classiest joint in town and then blow you in the restroom. She could cover your back in a bar fight and then discuss philosophy over a couple of martinis. Whatever it is it works. I know I have to see her. I toss the empty bottle at the side of the bridge and fire up my Caddy.

When I get to the Blue Room she's nowhere to be seen. The show is over and closing time looks just around the corner. I belly-up to the bar and start tossing back whiskey shots. I have no business drinking more liquor. But once the beast is loose it's best to let the critter run free. He sets them up and I knock them back. That's the way it goes for about twenty minutes. Hunched over the bar. Wasted. Chain-smoking Lucky's. Then I feel a tap on my shoulder. I turn and smile. Veronica is sitting beside me.

"Hey stranger. What brings you back so soon?"

"I'll give you two clues" I say. "She's got a voice like an angel and a body like an amusement park."

"Do you kiss your Mother with that potty mouth" she asks?

"You'd be surprised what I do with this mouth."

"You should suck on a bar of soap" she says. "That's what you should do with it."

"I tried that" I say. "It didn't work."

"Maybe you didn't suck hard enough" she says.

A dame with a mind as naughty as mine. I'm shocked. I'm speechless. I'm falling in love. I toss back another shot and clear my throat.

"You look like a million bucks tonight" I say.

"I wish I could say the same" she replies. "It looks like you've been ridden hard and put away wet."

"I wasn't that lucky."

"You want to tell me about it" she asks?

"What's to tell" I say? "Had a conversation with a crazy old man. Got chased through the streets by a psychopath in a Chevy. Then got drunk near some overpass downtown. Nothing too exciting. The usual."

"Sounds peachy" she says.

"More like a lemon if you ask me."

"I was always taught that when life deals you a lemon you should make lemonade."

"When life deals me a lemon I cut it into slices and stick them in my vodka Collins."

"Somehow that doesn't surprise me" she says. "How much have you drank tonight?"

"Enough to help me forget about the mess I'm in" I say.

"I don't get it" she says. "If it's such a mess why don't you just take off?"

"That's not my style" I say. "I didn't ask for all this. But I'm not going to turn my head and play dumb either. What about you? Why don't you hit the road and go see the world? What's your excuse for hanging around this dead-beat town?"

She pulls a Lucky from my pack and lights it up. She appears contemplative. Her eyes dark and brooding. The smoke creeps from her mouth like an extension of her. Demure. Sensual. Alive.

"I ran out of excuses a long time ago" she says. "I'm just a lonely girl trying to make some sense out of this crazy world."

"I don't buy it" I say. "Girls that look like you never get lonely."

"You'd be surprised."

"Well you don't have to be lonely tonight" I say.

"I got a hunch that's just the liquor talking."

"I got a hunch that's just your sobriety talking."

"Could be" she replies.

"Then let me buy you a drink."

"No thanks" she says.

"Why not" I ask?

"It's just one of those nights" she says. "One's too many and ten's not enough."

"Been there."

"Hey Buckley" she says after a short pause with her sexy eyes looking right through me.

"Yeah?"

"I know it's none of my business but I see a lot of sadness in your eyes. They're beautiful eyes but there's a lot of pain in them. You should let it out before it becomes too much."

Her words are harsh but also insightful. They seem to hurt and heal with equal strength. I feel vulnerable and weak. Nervous and embarrassed. But above all else I feel a deep and all consuming sadness. I close my eyes and fight back the sorrow.

When I open them up a few minutes later she's gone. Nothing remains save the lipstick-stained cigarette smoldering in the ashtray. I nurse one last nightcap then drop some change on the bar and roll to my hotel for some shuteye.

Late at night while I sleep I experience a haunting phenomenon. Memories floating up to me from the darkness like pretty balloons full of childhood fragments. But it isn't the dreams that disturb me. It's the space in which the dreams exist. Each memory is isolated. Disconnected. Broken off. I try to connect them. To fill in the gaps. No dice. Nothing but darkness. I hunt and hunt but all I find is more empty space. It feels as though my life is nothing more than a hodge-podge collection of second-rate memories tied together to create some bull-shit facade. Concealing a past that's as riddled with holes as a chump who got whacked with a Tommy gun.

I wake up terrified. Screaming and clutching the sheets. Sweating. Shaking. Sicker than a dog. I barely make it down the hall before the vomit comes out of my face. Kneeling on the floor with my elbows on the seat I stare down into yesterdays leftovers. And there in the yellow mess I see the face of Phillip Eckstein. It's purple and stiff and flies are landing in the bullet hole on his forehead. "I swear I don't know" he says. "All I know is that this town is not what it seems. Something isn't right." I flush the crapper and watch his purple face twist and gurgle down the porcelain orphace.

Down into the bowels of civilization. Where the dirty secrets go to die. Where all the shit and piss and jizz and blood get baptized and born again. Where the coat-hanger babies blow out candles on birthday cakes they never got to eat. Where the true American spirit courses through rusty pipes like blood through the veins of a diseased animal.

CHAPTER 5

▼

SILVER SPOONS AND BULLET WOUNDS

I can't tell if the noise is for real. Is someone at the door? Or is the pounding in my ears just the first stage of a vile and ruthless hangover? Concluding that the two are not mutually exclusive I open my eyes and attempt to wake up. The morning light grabs me by the ears and proceeds to skull fuck me mercilessly. "Who is it" I moan pulling the sheets back. No answer. Just more knocking. "Who the fuck is it?" Still no answer. I wrap the sheet around my naked body and crawl out of bed. "This better be good" I mumble as I open the door. Nobody. Just the junky hallway with its sad stories and its dead wallpaper. Then I see it. Taped to the door. A note. It reads "FAIR GROUNDS. FERRIS WHEEL. NINE O'CLOCK TONIGHT. YELLOW TIE. EYE PATCH. CANE."

I close my door and sit down on the bed. The whole thing is getting way out of hand. I liken my situation to one of those awkward yellows with a pig riding your ass. It's too late to stop. But to keep going means getting severely fucked. And so begins my day. Just another trip on the good ship monkey business.

I'm feeling extremely haggard and decide priority numero uno is to combat my hangover before it disables me entirely. I throw on some duds and stumble out into the day in search of some hair of the dog that bit me.

Word on the street is that Lucy's serves the stiffest drinks in town. It's your typical lowbrow titty club. A leather-faced tough guy working the door. A bygone broad pouring drinks. A dancer with a rock-hard body flashing her pink stinker with the mindless glee of a third grader at show and tell. A collection of drunks and pervs wasting to death in the smoky haze.

I order a bloody Mary and grab a seat next to the stage. The dancer is a young one. High titties and a hard rump. Well trimmed snatch and a squeaky clean asshole. She flips. She flops. She twirls around the pole like a tether ball at a popular playground.

I'm fascinated by the way this long-legged dame shakes her can in my face. There is something deep and far-out and mind-bending about it. She seems to embody the duality inherent in all things. She's contradiction incarnate. Ying yang in a platinum blonde wig. She's the American dream and the American nightmare. The product and the machine. The victim and the perpetrator. Silver spoons and bullet wounds.

The word on the street is legit. The drinks at Lucy's are stiff. Stiffer than a fourteen year olds pecker. And after a few more bloody Marys I'm feeling plenty high. But it's that weird creepy berserk kind of high. The kind of high when my thoughts are all big rusty anchors and my brain just can't stay afloat. It gets dragged down in the muck and starts going places it has no business going.

Like to Christmas morning 1932. Mom and Pops are crouched beside the tree. Pops is in his big green bathrobe. A cheap stogie is sticking out of his mouth. It bobs up and down as he does his best ho ho ho and points at all the presents. Mom waves her hand at the smoke. Wrinkles her nose. Pretends to cough. I stand in the hallway in my full-body pajamas. Blue. Fuzzy. Zipper down the middle. I run towards them. My little scuff-pad-feet gripping the hardwood floor. Then I jump into their arms and everything is safe and soft and good.

Because all thoughts of Mom and Dad lead back to the memory of their death. The look on the copper's face when he tells me they've been killed. The music in the church on the day of the funeral. The smell of Uncle Larry's aftershave. The way the sun shone on Grandma Wilder's bad orange wig. The sound of the dirt hitting their coffin lids. The endless nights of tortured sleep when their corpses would smile and hug me and tuck me in.

And all thoughts of death lead me to that woman. That poor woman. That woman whose name I don't even know. That woman who wouldn't stop walking toward me. That woman whose eye squirted me in the face like a God damned grapefruit. That woman who fell face down in front of me. Clawing at my legs. Smearing blood on my boots. That woman who wouldn't die but wasn't really alive. That woman who I had to put out of her misery with point blank shots to the back of her skull. That woman whose face I see in the faces of strangers on trains and in diners and in taxi cab windows.

And I'm left thinking about myself and my own inevitable death. Will my end be drawn out? Or will it arrive like so many teenage orgasms? Unexpectedly and far too soon. Will there be tubes in my nose keeping me alive like some freak show science fiction nightmare? Or will it end one night on the side of the highway with a pistol in my hand and a bottle of moonshine spilt at my feet? Does it even fucking matter? Once you hop that fence there's no getting back. And even the fullest of lives won't seem but a squirt in the bedpan of eternity.

By the time I leave the bar it's late afternoon. Time flies when you drink your lunch. The day has become unbearably hot. Fat broads with triple chins wave hand-held fans at their make-up caked faces. Old men with overalls and no teeth wipe at their greasy necks with heirloom handkerchiefs. Skinny little twerps suck coke bottles on the street corner and argue about what swimming hole to hit. It's all too much. My brain is feeling like a hardboiled egg. I know if I don't scram pronto I'll go stir crazy chasing my shadow through the heat wave streets. I beat cheeks back to the car and take a joy ride to cool off.

Out in the country I find a skinny patch of road that leads down to the Mississippi. I kick on a good jazz station and get out of the car and hunker down in the tall grass by the side of the river. The air is thick and sweet. Louis Armstrong is singing "Basin Street Blues." The sun is twinkling and dancing all over the river like little nursery rhyme stars drowning in the water. I close my eyes and let go of it all. I drift off to some place else. Some place safe and familiar. Lazy and nostalgic. Righteous and make-believe.

My dreams are all late August dreams. Summer dreams. Cherry pie twilights and barbecued hot-rods. Jazz record waves and cigarette sunburns. Baseball rope swings and drop-top bonfires. Cotton candy broads and neon orgasms. And somewhere in the middle of it all I see Veronica Vaughn. She's wearing high heel hubcaps and a Howdy Doody sundress. She's eating heart-shaped flap jacks at the diner of yesterday's dreams. She looks up at me and smiles and I can see eternity in her eyes.

I wake-up just after sunset. Kay Star is on the radio doing "Ain't Misbehaving." The sky is the color of cheap aluminum siding. The river is silent glass. Lightening bugs dance in the darkness. I fire up a smoke and sit up to watch the show. It's one of those cherry moments when everything is too cool for school and the monsters of disenchantment are crawling back under the bed where they belong. And I sit there with a shit-eating grin on my face feeling stupid and blessed. Knowing that the distance between myself and who I want to be has finally begun to recede.

It's getting to be that time. I pile in my Caddy and lay tracks toward the fairgrounds. It's good to be moving again. The nap has straightened me out and I feel like a million bucks.

I'm at the fairgrounds in no time flat. I park in a dirt lot by the highway and walk in. It's an ordinary county fair. The smell of hotdogs and popcorn. Beer and sweat. Sawdust and cow-shit. Country bumpkin kids displaying their pigs and bulls. Muscle-brained tough guys showing off for their old ladies by swinging a jack hammer to make the bell ring and the lights go flash. Little junior high space cadets shoving licorice and snow-cones into pimple-covered faces. Teenage sweethearts French kissing in the shadows. The big warped mirror making skinny people fat and fat people skinny. Industrial-strength slingshots twirling children through the balmy night.

Of course every beast has an underbelly. That which we try not to see. The carnies. The drunks. The bad seeds. A burnt-out cowboy with a busted leg and a past that he never mentions drinking whiskey beneath the big top. Some zombie-eyed carnie tearing tickets and staring up the skirts of little girls ridding the twirl-a-whirl. Couple of punks rolling a queer for loose change behind the ring toss.

I arrive at the Ferris wheel at nine o'clock. There's a line a mile long. But he's easy to spot. He stands out like a sore pecker. Bright yellow tie. Eye patch. Cane. Just like his note said.

"Hey mister" I ask. "You mind if I cut behind you?"

"Not at all" he replies.

He's old and skinny and stands hunched over. His get-up hangs from his bones like a sheet on a wash-line. He looks like a mix between some freakish bell-ringer character in a Victor Hugo novel and a Compton pimp.

When it's our turn the old fellow pays for two tickets and we both crawl in the cart. The giant wheel begins to creak and moan. Soon we're high above all the madness and filth. We're alone.

"Do you know who I am" he asks?

"Not a God damned clue."

"Well I know who you are" he says.

"What do you want a medal or something" I ask with a sneer?

"Calm down Whipper Snapper."

"My Grandma used to call me a Whipper Snapper" I say. "And you know what?"

"What" he asks?

"I didn't like it then and I don't like it now. The name's Buckley. Use it."

"Simmer down son" he says. "I didn't arrange this meeting to pick a fight."

"Then what did you do it for" I ask?

"To help you" he says.

"What are you my fucking fairy God father?"

"I'm afraid not."

"Then why" I ask?

"By helping you I will be helping myself" he says.

"What is it with this town? Everybody here talks in riddles. If you really want to help me you can cut the shit and give it to me straight."

"Very well" he says. "My name is Ralph Chambers."

"And what is it you want to tell me" I ask?

"I want to tell you that 'who would be born must first destroy a world. The bird flies to God.'"

"Well I'm sorry to tell you Ralph" I say. "But some other crazy old fuck already beat you to it. I got that line yesterday."

"I know you did" he says. "That's why I contacted you. Jarvis Beauchamp and I have known each other for a long time."

"How do you know I saw him" I ask?

"I know because I make it my business to know. I keep a keen eye on my old friend Jarvis."

"And why is that" I ask?

"As I'm sure you have discovered there is something wrong with this town. Jarvis Beauchamp knows what that is. Years ago when Jarvis was still relatively healthy he and I began to notice certain inconsistencies in the world around us. We became obsessed with understanding what was wrong with Shreveport. But unfortunately as we progressed so did Jarvis' disorder. Eventually we had to stop because we lost the means to communicate properly. However I have faith in Jarvis Beauchamp. He is an extremely intelligent fellow and I believe that not only has he solved the mystery surrounding this town but has also found away to work through his disorder. I believe his words hold the key. I believe he found that passage intentionally so that he might relay his ideas to others. I don't know where you came from Mr. Wilder. But I have a suspicion that you are a crucial part of all this."

"It doesn't matter where I came from" I say. "And it doesn't matter where I'm going either. All that matters is that I'm in Shreveport and I'm not leaving until I get to the bottom of all this."

"Well Mr. Wilder" he says slowly. "I want you to succeed. But I truly believe that your only hope is to take a closer look at the words of my friend Jarvis. I'm sure you know by now what book the passage is from. I suggest you get your hands on a copy. Perhaps you will be able to do what I can not. And that is understand what he is trying to tell us. Read it. Study it. Solve it. If you can understand his words you will get the answers you are looking for."

Down below the fairgoers move aimlessly through the maze. They appear like maggots swarming over a gigantic neon carcass. I can see herds of red blooded Americans spending their hard earned change on cheap thrills and greasy slop. Tossing rings on bottles. Chucking baseballs at bowling pins. Swinging rubber sledge hammers. All for a crack at the American dream. Or at least a big stuffed bunny.

"What do you know about a briefcase" I ask?

"Oh yes" he says. "The briefcase. I knew you would get to that eventually. Well I know that it is highly sought after."

"I already know that" I say. "Somebody's been shot because of it. My car's been busted into because of it. And some crazy fucker tried to run me off the road."

"It is true" he says. "There are some people out there who think reality can be solved by wealth or violence. Who think there is a short cut to enlightenment. That the contents of this particular briefcase could wipe away all their ignorance. Personally I believe in science. In philosophy. In intellectualism. I don't believe we need the briefcase to understand what is going on."

"Who are they" I ask?

"There's a man named William Blatt. He's obsessed with getting his hands on the briefcase. He has a couple of thugs working with him. There is an old guy by the name Red Johnson and a big Jewish guy named Phillip Eckstein. My advice to you is to avoid them. They are a ruthless bunch and they will not hesitate to hurt someone if it means getting what they want."

"Well I'll keep my eyes open for William Blatt" I say. "But I wouldn't worry about the other two. The last time I saw the old guy he was choking to death on his own blood. And as for Phillip Eckstein you'd need a cork to plug the bullet hole in his forehead."

And on that note our Ferris wheel ride comes to an end.

It's late when I leave the fair. The streets are dead and I'm not much better. Darkness is everywhere. Sunk in deep like a greedy tic that won't let go. Count Baise is on the radio doing "Money is Honey." I light a Lucky Strike and roll through the silent streets trying to unravel the knot in my brain.

I'm starting to feel that I might have bit off more than I can chew. There are more pieces to the puzzle than I had thought and the picture that's forming is not a pretty one. Something big is coming from over the horizon and I have a hunch that when it rears its ugly head there's going to be a lot of fuckers caught with their cheese in the wind. But what was this dirty little secret? And why was someone so bent on keeping it hush-hush?

The city is a junkyard and we're just a pack of starving dogs fighting for the role of king shit. We're all after the same thing. We just don't know what it is. But we know we need it. And I need to get it first. That's just who I am. The type of fellow who always plays for keeps when it comes to skin and bone.

But am I ready for the burden of discovery? It's easy to ask the questions. But am I man enough to stomach the answers? Am I willing to dig up the truth even if it means an epiphany that could cause my brain to pop like a pimple?

I've heard a lot of strange talk. Shady stories. Paranoid rants. Most of it's like week-old Chinese food. It's hard to swallow and doesn't settle right. Flaws in reality? Glitches in the city? It sounds like a bucket of donkey shit to me. But there is a certain something that I just can't ignore. A sincerity in their voices. A fear in their eyes. It isn't that I don't believe them. It's that I don't want to believe them. Too many frightening implications.

Red Johnson. Phillip Eckstein. William Blatt. Jarvis Beauchamp. Ralph Chambers. Who are all these people? And more importantly who am I to them? There is something different about all of us. Something that separates us from the hordes of average Joes roaming the sidewalks. It feels as though we're all caught in some collective web of self discovery. The only question is who is the fiend who spun the web?

I finish my smoke and flick the butt out the window. The knot in my brain won't unravel and the more I tug the tighter it gets. On the radio is Henry 'Red' Allen. The tune is "Pleasin' Paul." I crank the volume and gun it for home.

I'm a mile from the hotel when I see the son of a bitch who tried to run me off the road. He's easy to spot. One head light. Smashed fender. I kill the lights and park in the shadows. When I'm sure he hasn't seen me I whip a U-turn and start tailing him. I don't have a plan. I just know I need some answers. And I have a hunch the knuckle-head in the Chevy can give me some.

I hang back a ways. Loose. Inconspicuous. Crouched low in the seat like a gang-banger from East L.A. Rolling stealth. Checking it all out. Following him like a ghost. A rumor. A lazy shadow.

He leads me to some industrial area outside of town. All is dead. All is beat. All is creepy switching-yards and vacant intersections. Whatever industry had prompted the development has long since gone under.

He cuts across some railroad tracks and turns down a dead-end alley. I coast to a stop then get out and peer around the corner. He's parked next to a rundown warehouse. An old building that's nothing but a hotel for rats and cockroaches. A bottom of the barrel crash-pad for drunks and junkies. He gets out of his car and enters the building.

I don't like the scene. There's a funny vibe in the air. Feels like shit could go hay-wire at the drop of a hat. My gut tells me to split but I ignore it. I haven't come this far to tuck my tail between my legs and scamper off like a dog that pissed on an electric fence. I grab my gun out of the glove box and start creeping down the alley.

I'm nearing his Chevy when I hear a voice. It's coming from the trunk. My heart skips a beat and my stomach jumps up in my throat. I stop. Cock my piece. Listen. It's a woman's voice. It's calling for help. It's familiar.

With adrenalin surging through my veins like diesel through a tricked-out V-8 I jump into action. I run to the driver's window and look in. Bingo. The keys are dangling from the ignition. I pop open the trunk. My jaw drops. It's Veronica Vaughn. Hog-tied. Gagged. Her eyes bulging with fear. Her face sweaty. Her lips trembling. Her body flailing like a child's.

For just a second I let my eyes fall across her body. I know it's inappropriate. I know it's not the time. But I can't help myself. Even under the oddest of circumstances I'm a man first and foremost. She's wearing a black sequined dress. Her arms are tied behind her back. It causes her breasts to push forward. Big. Round. Heavy looking. They barely fit inside her dress. And the dress is torn and twisted. Bunched up around the waist. Her legs are exposed from top to bottom. They're long and lean and milky-white. All of this I see in a heart beat.

I stick the piece in the small of my back and loosen her gag. She starts to scream but I cover her mouth.

"Shh" I whisper as I go to work untying her. "It's me Buckley. You're safe now. I got you."

"He was in my house" she cries hysterically. "I tried to get away but…"

"Veronica" I say as I lean in and scoop her up out of the trunk. "You need to listen to me closely. Here are the keys to my car. It's parked around the corner. I want you to take it and get out of here. I'm staying in a little dive downtown. 1137 Chelsea Street room 508. You'll be safe there."

"What about you" she asks? "What are you going to do?"

But I don't say a thing. I just draw my piece and head toward the building. The place is bad news. It stinks like rodent shit. I can almost feel their beady little eyes watching me from the darkness. I move to the end of the hallway and look around the corner.

There's a large room. A light bulb hangs from the ceiling. It flickers a dull yellow. A mattress. A torn up couch. A beat-up end table. There's a pack of smokes and a newspaper. And under the newspaper I can see a handgun.

I hear a voice and look up. There's a man in the far corner. His back is to me. He's hunched over a hot-plate stirring a pot of canned soup. He's humming and singing to himself. A small and wiry looking fellow. Black hair greased back. Sharp get-up. Collared shirt. Pinstripe slacks and vest. Typical gangster duds.

I stick my piece in the small of my back and walk into the room. Soft steps. Not a sound. I quietly pick up his gun from under the newspaper. It's a .45 automatic. After emptying the chamber I pop the clip and empty it too. I put the bullets in my pocket then put the gun on the table where I found it. I walk over to the couch and sit down.

"I've got a phone number I could give you" I say after a few minutes of watching him cook and sing and sip his soup.

"And what number is that" he asks spinning around and trying not to look startled?

"It's the number to a good body shop" I say as I pull a Lucky from my pack and fire it up. "Looks like that Chevy of yours got a little banged up."

"I'd take my Chevy over that Cadillac of yours any day of the week."

"Sure you would asshole."

"Fuck you" he says.

"You wish faggot" I reply as he strolls over and takes a seat beside me on the couch.

For the first time I get a good look at his face. It's handsome. But not a good handsome. A mean handsome. It's too devilish. Too cruel. Too ruthless. Strong jaws. Sharp nose. Small mouth. Squinty eyes. Tight skin. His is the look of a fallen angel. A one time boy scout turned violent hood.

"Nice place you got here" I say. "You decorate it yourself?"

"Can the comedy act" he says. "We both know why you're here. You're here to play hero for your little gal pal Veronica Vaughn. I know you want a piece of that ass. And I knew you'd jump at the chance to play captain-save-the-day. I was just using her for bait. You're who I want. We need to talk. You got something of mine. I suggest you give it to me."

"Well Sherlock" I say. "You're right about one thing. I do want to bang Veronica Vaughn. But believe me this has nothing to do with her. This is just between you and me."

"Well where is it" he asks?

"You're barking up the wrong tree William Blatt."

"Someone's done his homework" he says. "But it doesn't matter. Everything you think you know doesn't mean shit."

"Are you telling me you're not William Blatt" I ask?

"Maybe" he says. "Maybe not. It depends."

"On what" I ask?

"Fuck if I know" he says. "It just depends."

"I don't get it."

"I'm not surprised" he says. "You're new to this town. You don't know what's going on."

"You're right. I don't" I say. "Why don't you tell me."

"It's not that easy. There's no simple explanation. There's no rules. No answers. No rhyme or reason. Just disorder. Nonsense. Fucking chaos."

"And you hope that whatever is in the briefcase will explain things."

"That's the idea" he says.

"Is that why you killed Phillip Eckstein? Because you thought he was making off with the goods?"

"How do you know I killed him" he asks?

"He's murdered. You're a heartless little weasel. Call it an educated guess."

"Well you're a regular Dick Tracy aren't you? You're right though" he says. "I did kill him. Or did I? It's hard to tell."

"And why's that" I ask?

"Because it's hard to kill somebody if they don't actually exist."

"Don't feed me that far-fetched bullshit" I say. "I was there. I saw his brains on the bed. I smelt the blood."

"Did you? Did you really? Then why was there nothing about it in the papers? Why is there no record of it? Feel free to look. You won't find shit."

"I know what I saw" I say. "And I know you tried to run me off the road. And I know I'm about sick and tired of you meddling in my shit. Now I know there's some deep shit going on around here and you best believe I'm sticking around until I get to the bottom of it. My advice to you is stay the fuck out of my way or my next visit won't be so pleasant."

He lunges off the couch and grabs his gun from the end table. He thinks I hadn't seen it. He thinks he's one upped me. He thinks he's Humphrey fucking Bogart.

"Who do you think you're fucking with" he asks? "You think I'm a pussy? You think you can scare me? You think you can just bullshit me and then walk out of here alive? I don't think so. But I'm going to give you one more chance. I'm going to ask you one more time. Where's the briefcase?"

"Go fuck your mother" I say as I rub out my cigarette in the ashtray.

"Please" he says. "Say it again. Say it one more time. I would love to put a bullet right through your face."

"Go fuck your mother."

"Don't think I won't do it" he says. "I will blow your brains right the fuck out. Now where the fuck is it?"

"Go fuck your mother."

"Fuck you you piece of shit" he roars as he steps toward me with the gun pointed at my head. "I will fuck you up. I will destroy you. Now I'm just going to ask one last time you filthy cock sucker. And I swear to God if you say that again I'm going to put so many god damned bullets in your head your skull will sound like a fucking baby rattle. Now where the fuck is the briefcase?"

"Go fuck your mother" I say calmly.

His fury erupts. He snaps. He goes ape shit. He puts the gun to my forehead and starts pulling the trigger. But he's so blind with hate and rage that he can't tell he's been duped. He just stands there looking like an ass. Pulling the trigger over and over. Eventually he stops. He lowers his gun. His shoulders slouch. His expression is sad and pathetic.

"Two flies were sitting on top of a lawnmower" I say as I reach behind my back and pull out my revolver. "Just relaxing by the barnyard when a steer strolls by and drops a huge pile of shit. The two flies swoop down and eat some of it then fly back up to the lawn mower handle. One fly said "that was really good. I think I'll have some more. You want to come with me?" "No thanks" said the other fly. So the fly goes down and eats some more. Afterwards he can barely get back up to the lawnmower handle because he was stuffed with shit. But he still wanted more. "That stuff is just too good" he said. "I think I might eat some more. Are you sure you don't want to come with me?" "I'm sure" replied the other fly. So the fly goes down for more. But he's too stuffed. He's so fat and heavy that he just falls right to the ground and splatters."

"What's the fucking point" William Blatt demands?

"The point" I say. "Is that you shouldn't fly off the handle if you're full of shit."

And then I clock him across the face with my revolver. His cheek splits to the bone and he drops like a bag of dirt. I kneel on his chest and keep wailing on him. Soon his face resembles a bag of rotten tomatoes. But I can't stop. I keep laying into him. Harder and harder. Over and over. Until there's nothing but blood and bone and gristle. But still I can't stop. I beat his face until there's no face left at all. And then I beat it some more. All my violent tendencies have been repressed too long and are suddenly in full revolt. They come flowing out of me like a spontaneous poem. And my poem is about the nature of man. My poem is about that fine line between beast and angel. My poem is about the jungle and the lion and the law of nature. My poem is about the bloody highway of self-discovery. My poem is about a stupid piece of trash who pushed me too far and got fucking beat to death in a dirty old warehouse.

It's a long walk to the hotel. By the time I arrive the horizon is the pale color of early dawn. I find Veronica in my bed sound asleep. I can see the outline of her body under the covers. I stand there a while and admire it. She looks like an exotic butterfly too cozy to leave the cocoon. I resist the urge to lie down on the bed and make some clumsy pass at her. The timing isn't right. Plus I'm so exhausted I wouldn't be worth two hoots in the sack. So I lie down on the floor. Before I know it I'm out cold.

As always my sleep is twisted and disturbed. I dream I'm getting gang-banged by a platoon of Korean soldiers on a bed covered with sheets made from the skin of dead marines. For two days straight I endure their greasy little chink pricks stabbing my guts until eventually I pass out from the pain. When I wake up I'm a finch locked inside a cage built from my parent's bones and Herman Hesse is standing outside watching me. He holds a bowl of water and a copy of Demian. He slips the bowl into my cage but as I drink the water it turns into my parent's blood and as I drink their blood I become aware of my own consciousness. Herman Hesse understands this and unlocks the cage and as I fly away I can hear him reading aloud from his book. And I fly and fly but then I hear a blast and look down to see the ghost of the one-eyed peasant woman holding a smoking shotgun. When I hit the ground I'm already dead and I'm at my own funeral. The peasant woman has pulled out my eyeballs and stuck them with toothpicks and is serving them as appetizers to my family and friends. Everyone is sobbing and hugging and eating my eyeballs while President Truman sings the national anthem. Then they drape an American flag over my coffin and lower it into the dirt. But I notice it isn't a coffin at all but a gigantic briefcase. Then it's all dark and I'm inside the briefcase and someone is carrying me. When it opens I see Veronica Vaughn and we are alone in a fancy hotel room on our honeymoon. I step out of the briefcase and move toward the bed where she lays on her back with her legs spread. I drop to my knees and start giving her oral when suddenly I realize I'm not eating a pussy but coming out of one. And as I'm born I recognize the doctor as the guy I beat to death and his face is all smashed and hideous. He says "you can't kill someone if they don't exist" and then he slits my throat with a scalpel and I die having never really lived at all.

CHAPTER 6

▼

TWO HUNDRED POUNDS
OF LUST AND MUSCLE

I wake up in a sad mood. I can't put my finger on why. It's just one of those days when the sun doesn't look right slanting in through the window. One of those days when your heart hurts for every reason all at once. One of those days when the world outside sounds like the saddest jazz song ever heard. One of those days when the air smells like death.

Veronica Vaughn is long gone. She's left a note on the bed. It thanks me for saving her and invites me over for dinner. I crumble it up and throw it on the floor. I walk over to the window and stand there staring out. Everything looks strange and out of whack. The sky and the earth look like siblings that can't get along but have to sit next to each other at thanksgiving dinner. I step away from the window and sit down on the bed. I feel a sadness coming on hard.

Pretty soon I start feeling cooped up. Stir-crazy. I get dressed and split. I take a long walk. I do a lot of thinking. How long have I been back in the states? A week? Two weeks? Already my life has become a distorted version of what I had envisioned. I had planned on proposing to Susan. But her cheating ass has become just a distant memory. One of those people who cease to exist except when I'm sloppy drunk and the past comes rushing at me from the darkness like a bum with a thousand faces and a switchblade the size of a Pontiac. One of those people who get folded up like an old love letter and put in the box in the back of my mind. Enter Veronica Vaughn. Completely out of nowhere. Sweeping me right off my feet. And so goes life. Flames burn out like forgotten candles. Friends get replaced like last years toys. Faces come and go. Tear drops fall. Meat decomposes. And everything's cool so long as the monkeys and piss-ants don't get hip to the game.

I come across the Shreveport public library. I decide to get a copy of Demian. I take the stairs two at a time. Typical scene inside. Quiet. Musty smelling. Geeks and book-worms wall to wall. Old dame librarian watching everyone like a bull-dog. I make my way to the fiction section. Start hunting. Alcott. Byron. Conrad. Dostoyevsky. Ellison. Fitzgerald. Gogol. I hit the H's and cross my fingers. Hardy. Hawthorne. Hemmingway. Huxley. No dice. A whole mess of H's just not the right one. I head up front. The old broad at the desk watches me approach with distrusting eyes.

"Can I help you sir?"

"I hope so. I'm looking for Demian by the German author Herman Hesse."

"It should be against the far wall" she says pushing her glasses up the bridge of her nose. "In the fiction section."

"I just looked" I say. "It wasn't there."

"Well I know we carry it" she says. "If it's not on the shelf it must be checked out. Would you be interested in another of his novels? I believe we have a few."

"There wasn't any out there" I say.

"Really? Perhaps they've all been checked out."

"Would you mind seeing if that's the case" I ask?

"One moment" she says rolling her eyes.

"What's the verdict" I ask a moment later as she returns to her desk wearing an amused expression?

"It's peculiar" she says.

"What's that" I ask?

"That they're all checked out by the same person."

"You're right" I say as I walk out scratching my chin. "That is peculiar."

Back on the streets. Chain smoking. Digging dreary scenes on a late summer day. Thinking about my country. About the ways it has changed while I was off at war. Something is different. But what? Has something new been acquired? Or has something fundamental been lost? No way of telling. I just know the times are changing.

The new cars aren't as boss. More style less meat. Jazz is changing too. Swing is out and bop is in. Civil rights are heating up. Hoola-hoops are the latest thing. The Korean war is just another crowbar for the jack-off's in Washington to gain political leverage. And all across the nation the great commie witch hunt is taking shape.

But all this is just pop culture bullshit. Crap that we'll teach the kiddies twenty years down the road in history class. The real change is seen in the people. The real change is occurring beneath the surface. Where the magma of our society churns and gurgles and flips ambiguous birds at the people up top. It's in the people's gestures. It's in the way people blow the smoke out after a drag on their cigarette. It's in the way they walk to work. It's in the way they scarf their food. It's in the color of their shit. It's in the sound of their orgasms.

I keep walking and soon I come across a used book store. I decide to try my luck again. It's a stuffy little joint. Dark. Dusty. Cluttered. An old Chinese fellow sporting a ponytail and a fu manchu sits behind the counter sucking on a pipe. A green-eyed cat with mangy fur is snoozing belly up in the window sill. A small rodent skull sits on the counter and holds a burning stick of incense.

"What's happening" I ask strolling in?

The old man looks up at me with glazy eyes then turns his attention back to his pipe. I make my way through the maze of hardbacks. Despite the poor lighting and general disorder I find some Herman Hesse lickety-split. I grab a copy of Demian and take it up front.

"Paperback fifteen cent" says the old fellow behind the counter.

I fight back some chuckles because I'm reminded of a stupid rhyme my Dad used to say when I was a kid. Ching Chong Chinaman sitting on a fence trying to make a dollar out of fifteen cents. I drop a couple of coins and stroll out with a shit-eating grin on my face.

Walking back to the hotel I see a cafe and duck inside for a cup of coffee to go. The place is cozy. Has a French feel. I decide to stay. Do some reading. I grab a table by the window and open my book.

It's near shot. Tattered as hell. One of those hardbacks that looks as if it has passed through a hundred different hands. It's nostalgic. Makes me think of L.A. in the 30's. I was a kid and I'd swipe a dime off my old man's dresser and run to the corner store and grab some trashy crime novel. I'd hunker down at the malt shop and kill entire days. Happy and content.

I finish a few chapters. I look out the window. The streets have grown dark. Nighttime has arrived. I think of Veronica Vaughn and my dinner invitation. I smile. Bunny-ear the page. Take off.

On my way to her pad I pick up a couple bottles of wine and a fresh pack of Lucky's. I'm there in a red hot minute. I find her name and press the button. The door buzzes. I let myself in and head up the stairs in the direction of where I remember seeing her in the window.

When the door opens I feel as though I've fallen into a dream. A fantasy that I have no business being a part of. There stands Veronica Vaughn. Hotter than a car engine going over the grape vine pass on a scorching day in August. She's wearing a sexy pink blouse. A gray wool skirt hanging just below the knees. Black shoes with shiny little buckles. Her hair is pulled up in a bun except for one wavy strand that hangs down along the side of her face. She's holding a bowl and stirring it with a big wooden spoon. She looks flawless as always.

"You going to stand there all night gawking" she asks? "Or are you going to come in and help me cook dinner?"

"I haven't quite decided."

She turns and I follow her in. Her apartment is eclectic. Part Grandma and Grandpa's place. Part junky crash pad. Nice rugs on hardwood floors. Ashtrays piled high with butts. A red velvet divan. Neon Budweiser sign hanging on the wall. A record player. A reading chair. An assortment of strange and peculiar knick-knacks. Dolls. Lunch pails. Toys. Trinkets.

I stop by the front window and stare outside. Nighttime Shreveport is alive with lights. Bars. Diners. Bowling alleys. Nudey joints. Traffic racing through the city. And across the street I see the dumpy apartment where Phillip Eckstien got whacked. I shake his image from my mind and continue into the kitchen.

"What are we cooking" I ask setting the wine bottles down?

"It's supposed to be fettuccini alfredo with chicken breasts covered in a sautéed mushroom sauce. But what it actually ends up being I have no idea. I'm not exactly a good cook. I just couldn't think of how else to say thank you."

"You don't have to thank me" I say. "It's all in a days work."

"Who was he" she asks?

"His name's William Blatt" I say. "He was just a no good hood trying to get his hands on that God damned briefcase. But I have a strong hunch he won't be bothering you anymore. I don't think he'll be bothering anybody anymore."

"What did he want with me anyway" she asks?

"It wasn't you he wanted. It was me. He thought I'd come to the rescue if I knew you were in trouble."

"Why would he think that" she asks?

"He was under the impression that I wanted to get inside your pants."

"Is that true" she asks?

"Of course not. That's ridiculous. There's no way I could fit inside your pants."

She blushes and turns away. She cooks. I watch. She has a body you could bounce a quarter off of. Her neck is lean and her pretty hair sits on top like a blossoming flower. Her skirt fits her ass like store-bought skin. Her legs are like an expensive steak. Lean but with plenty of meat.

"Buckley" she asks? "How did you really get tangled up in all of this? What's your story?"

"It's a long one" I say.

"Well dinner's not ready yet" she says. "Let's hear it."

"Well I guess I'm here because of some Korean's skill at hiding landmines" I say. "I was fighting overseas. A fellow in my platoon named Blanchard triggered an explosion and I caught some of the blast in my side. Nothing too serious but it got me sent home. I had a girl back in L.A.. At least I thought I did. When I got back I caught her shacked up with some grease-ball. I decided it was a good time to start over. I bought a Cadillac and took off. Headed east. Couple of days later I was passing through Texas when the car in front of me crashed into a field. I got out to help and the old guy behind the wheel asked if I could get his briefcase to Shreveport. He died a minute later and I decided to go ahead and bring it here."

"And here you are" she says.

"And here I am."

"And what have you found here in Shreveport" she asks?

"A whole lot of nothing" I reply. "Phillip Eckstien was the fellow I was supposed to give the briefcase to. But when I arrived at his place I found him dead as a doornail. I ran outside to find my trunk wide open and the briefcase gone. That's when I saw you. We met later that night and you mentioned a guy named Jarvis Beauchamp. The next day I found out where he lives and took a drive out to meet him. The guy was two sandwiches short of a picnic. All he could do was quote Herman Hesse and jump around like an orangutan. Then I left his place and on the way home some psychopath tried running me off the road. The next morning I found a note on my door inviting me to the fair. When I showed up I met some guy named Ralph Chambers. He's friends with Jarvis Beauchamp. He told me that the answers to all my questions were in the words that Jarvis spoke. He told me to go get a copy of the book Demian and read it. And then on my way home I spotted the guy who tried to run me off the road. I tailed him all the way out to the river. That's where I found you. After pulling you out of the trunk I headed inside and had a little chat. That's when I met this Mr. Blatt. He confessed to killing Phillip Eckstien because he thought he was making off with the briefcase. He told me there's something wrong with this city. Something really wrong. Then he asked me where the briefcase was and when I told him to go fuck his mother he went crazy and pulled a gun and tried to kill me. I beat him until he stopped fighting back then went home and went to sleep. I woke up this morning feeling depressed as hell. Walked around all day. Bought a copy of that Herman Hesse book. And here I am."

"Well you're right" she says. "That is a long story. I think I need a drink after all that. And by the sound of it you could use one too."

"Thanks" I say as I uncork the first bottle and pour a couple glasses. "So let's hear your story."

"Yours is a hard act to follow" she says. "My story is boring compared to that. I grew up here in Shreveport in a foster home. Spent my early years wishing I hadn't developed so fast. And spent the last few years wishing I looked the way I did back then. Grass is always greener sort of thing. All I got going now is my gig at the Blue Room. Just singing there a few nights a week. Trying to make ends meet."

"Why don't you get out of here" I ask? "With a voice like yours you could make it anywhere."

"Oh believe me I've thought about it" she says. "I just never follow through. I guess I'm scared or lazy or something. Nowadays it's all I can do just to keep myself together. Keep in touch with reality."

"You know what" I say raising my glass. "To hell with reality. Reality's just a crutch for people who can't handle drugs."

"You're right" she says laughing and clinking her glass against mine. "To hell with reality."

When dinner is ready we move to the dinning room. That's where the evening begins to flow. Ambiance is thick. Dinner is delicious. Conversation is natural. We laugh. We smile. We ride a wicked wine buzz. And all the while I stare in awe at the beauty of Veronica Vaughn. But it's more than her beauty. She seems to glow with an almost unbearable sexual energy. Every gesture is indicative. Every glance arousing. Every smile seductive. And I know I'm not alone in my longing. There's a hunger in her eyes. I can see it as surely as a male dog can smell a bitch in heat from a block away. But it's all unspoken. And that's why it's so arousing. Nothing but red wine and body language. Just sparks and giggles and killer vibes.

Shortly after dinner I get up to take a leak. I cut through the living room toward the hallway. On the floor beside the record player I see a stack of jazz albums two feet high. I take a quick piss then hurry back to the living room. I hunker down on the floor and start flipping through the pile. I feel like a kid in a candy store. They're all my old favorites. Charlie Barnett. Buster Bailey. Cab Calloway. Dizzy Gillespie. Earl Hines. Jelly Roll Morton. Red Nichols. Djengo Reinhardt. Fats Waller. Mugsy Spainer.

"Veronica" I yell. "You've got some amazing music here."

"Thanks" she says walking into the room.

"Can we play one" I ask?

"Of course."

So I grab an old Coleman Hawkins record and toss it on. The music is magical. It fills the room with a feeling. An emotion. A mood so heavy it's damn near palpable. It puts into sound all the lustful thoughts that I can not voice. It articulates all my romantic desires.

"Can I have this dance" I ask stepping toward Veronica?

"I don't know" she replies hesitantly. "I can sing like a bird but I can't dance to save my life."

"Me neither" I say. "We'll be a match made in heaven."

Then she steps into my embrace. We float across the floor. Smooth. Easy. Effortless. The only light is from the beer sign hanging on the wall. It gives the scene a dreamy vibe. We become one with the music. We drift through the neon haze. We stare into each other's eyes. We smile like brand new children.

"I feel safe in your arms" she says.

"You are safe" I whisper. "As long as you're with me nobody's going to hurt you. I promise."

"It's not people I'm afraid of" she says. "It's me."

"What do you mean" I ask?

"I just don't know if I can do it anymore" she says. "Sometimes life's just too much. Sometimes I can't tell what's real and what's not."

"Look at me" I say lifting her chin with my finger. "Look me in the eyes. Right here. Right now. This is real."

Time stands still as we gaze into each other's eyes. Then our lips meet. It's short and sweet. But in those few seconds a spark is born. And that spark becomes a raging flame. By the time we pull apart to catch our breath our lust is at a fever pitch. We go at it again. This time no pussy-footing. Serious business right off the bat. Lips locked hard. Bodies pressed tight. Hearts beating fast.

"You make me feel so amazing" she says in a husky whisper.

"You haven't seen anything yet."

And then more kissing. Wild. Savage. Uninhibited. I move my hands down the small of her back. Her spine is like a string of tiny pebbles. And when I reach her ass I don't hesitate to grab a handful. I squeeze hard. She lets out a moan and her eyes roll back. I pull hard on her ass. Rubbing myself against her. She catches on quick. Takes charge. Begins thrusting her hips against mine. We fall into a frenzied motion. Forceful. Urgent. I pull her hair back and kiss her neck like crazy.

"I want you so bad" I say. "I want you. I want you. I want you."

"You have me" she says. "You have me. You have me. You have me."

And that's what finally does it. Her voice. Not the wine. Not the jazz. Not the dancing. It's just the sound of her sultry voice talking sexy in my ear. All my composure goes right out the window. I'm reduced to the core of my nature. Nothing but two hundred pounds of lust and muscle.

I pull her blouse wide open. Buttons pop off in so many directions. Her eyes bulge with alarm and excitement. Shock and delight. But beneath the kicks and thrills is an acceptance. A submission. An understanding that she is mine entirely. To have and to do with as I choose.

She arches her shoulders and her blouse falls to the floor. She then reaches behind her back and unsnaps her bra. It slips off her like discarded skin. I just stand there taking it all in. The hair cascading over her shoulders. The slender waist. The slope of her belly. And those tits. My God those tits. Larger than I ever could have thought. Enormous and round. Nipples perky and erect.

"If you like them so much" she says. "Why don't you touch them."

And so I do. First with my hands. Then with my mouth. Greedy and ravenous. Squeezing. Sucking. Licking. Biting.

"How do you want me" she moans?

"Turn around" I say. "Hands on the wall."

She does as she's told. Hands high on the wall. Legs spread as far as her skirt will allow. I come up behind her. Kissing the back of her neck. Grabbing her breasts. Smelling her hair. I lick my way down her back. Her muscles flex and tighten. Her whole body writhes. Vibrates. Buzzes. In one quick and violent motion I yank her skirt up to her waist. She's wearing panties and stockings and a garter. All white. I pull her panties down to the floor. I kiss her bare flesh. Rub her thighs. Squeeze her ass cheeks.

I stand up. Rip my shirt off. Unbutton my Levis. Drop them to my knees. My cock is so hard I think the skin is going to rip. I've never seen it this large. The size of a God damned Louisville Slugger. Veins like ropes under my skin. Head swollen and purple. I spit on my cock. It glistens. I place my hands under her ass. Lift and spread. The tip of my penis feels her opening. I enter her. Not gentle. Not bit by bit. But all at once. Hard and forceful. She lets out a scream. I grip her ass with both hands. I spread her cheeks. I watch my cock slide in and out.

Her hair hangs down to the small of her back. I grab it and yank. Pulling myself into her. Deeper. Faster. A wild pace. Her ass slaps loud. Sweat covers our bodies. We cry out in pleasure.

When I feel myself nearing climax I slow down. It feels too good to end this soon. I pull out and step back. Veronica turns and faces me. I've never seen anything so hot in my life. Hair wild and messy. Tits glistening. Skirt bunched up around her waist. Mascara running down her sweaty face. Lip stick smudged. She's all woman and she knows it. She rejoices in the knowledge that she possesses everything I desire. Tits. Cunt. Ass. Mouth. These are hers and she's proud.

She gets on her knees in front of me and grabs my cock.

"How do you want it" she asks?

"Put it in your mouth as deep as you can."

She does it slowly so I can watch. Staring me straight in the eyes. Inch by inch. Deeper and deeper. Until every bit of me is inside her. Then she pulls it out and gasps for breath. Saliva hanging from her chin.

"Now do it fast" I say. "As fast as you can."

She goes at it crazy. Wild. Freaky. Like a retarded kid with a lolly pop. For minutes on end she works it at a break-neck pace. My cock burns with pleasure. Then she stops. Looks up at me like a starving animal. Turns over onto her hands and knees.

I get on the floor behind her. Slip my cock inside her. I start in nice and slow. Squeezing her ass hard. Spreading her cheeks wide. Staring at her tight little asshole. Pushing in as deep as I can go. Pulling out until I could see the head. Pushing it in again. Over and over. Then my pace quickens. She arches her back and starts flopping her hair all over. Sweat drips from my nose onto the small of her back. We both yell with ecstasy. We both let go and drift away to a land of pure pleasure.

"Get on top of me" she says as she rolls over on to her back. "I want to look in your eyes when I come."

She lays there on her back. Legs spread wide apart. Pussy soaking wet. I take a moment just to let it sink in. It's magical and obscene. Appalling and terrific. When I can't take it anymore I fall on her and go to town. All out. As hard as I can. My hands on her ankles. Her ankles by her ears. Deep penetration. Wicked pace. Tits bouncing. Balls slapping. Mouth quivering. Sweat flying. Ass clapping. Nails scratching. Teeth grinding. Muscles rippling. Everything all at once in a prolonged scream of sexual liberation. And then she gets a crazed look in her eyes and I know she's achieved the big O. Every muscle in her body flexes at once. A high pitched scream fills the entire room. She twitches. She spasms. She stares me dead in the eyes with an intensity that transcends the moment. She lets her orgasm take her. And in doing so exposes her individuality to me. Shamelessly. Uninhibitedly. Boldly.

Watching her come is too much for me. Too exciting. Too stimulating. It pushes me over the edge of no return. I feel a tremendous tingling in my balls. I pull out as my orgasm hits full force. My body goes numb with ecstasy. But still it grows and grows. More and more intense until I think I'm going to explode. So much pleasure and it's all being channeled through the tip of my cock. I look down just as the cum begins to shoot out. Veronica grabs my cock and begins stroking it violently.

"Oh God fuck" I yell as my cum flies everywhere. "Oh shit. Oh shit."

Her stomach. Her tits. Even her face. My cum covers her completely. But still there's more. She milks it dry. Every last drop.

I collapse on top of her. Exhausted. My cum warm and wet between our naked bodies. I kiss her mouth and taste my own juice. I try to speak but no words occur. So I close my eyes and lower my head. I enjoy the moment for what it is. Whatever it is.

Shortly afterwards we're in her bedroom. Lying down. Entwined. Her head on my shoulder. Smoking cigarettes in the darkness. A jazz record playing quietly in the other room. Through the window we can see the faint traces of morning. Turning the horizon a dingy purple.

"Can I share a secret with you" I ask between drags on my Lucky Strike?

"Of course" she says.

"I masturbated to you the first night we met."

"You're kidding" she says after a short pause. "That's too funny. I masturbated to you the first night we met."

We laugh and kiss and feel round two coming on.

CHAPTER 7

▼

THE DARK AND CROOKED SIDEWALKS OF A FACELESS AMERICA

This is how things go for a stretch. Autumn moves in. Summer is on the skids. Dark clouds hang low in the sky like a bad mood. Days drift away like time elapsing in a Hollywood movie. A fan. A calendar. Pages turned by invisible fingers. Shorter days. Longer nights. Red leaves on the dirty ground. Empty trees with bone finger branches. Fog crawls through the glistening streets. Rain drips from the eaves. Car tires hiss. Neon lights glitter in the puddles.

Along with the weather I too start changing. Becoming darker. Colder. Harder. Obsessed. Pacing my shit hole like a windup toy robot. Chain-smoking Lucky's. Air so thick with smoke you can't cut it with a chainsaw. Ashtrays like toxic flowers blossoming with stale butts. Pulling my hair out in frustration because I can't wrap my mind around the gist of it all. Dipping. Weaving. Bobbing. Shadowboxing with the facts. Laying on the bed. Staring at the ceiling. A cigarette in my mouth with ash two inches long. Smoking reefer and eating Benzedrine that I bought off a Mexican staying in a room at the end of the hall. Getting high as hell. Bouncing off the walls. Digging the razor sharp edge. The tight nerves. The big eyes. The twitchy high-strung energy. Doing push-ups with a joint in my mouth. Sit-ups. Pull-ups. Keeping lean. Keeping the blood pumping. Working off the nervous high.

Fighting off my past when it rears its haggard face. The time in Korea still haunts me. Working watch in the middle of the night. Clutching my rifle with shaky hands. Sweat stinging my eyes. Shitting my drawers every time a cricket chirps. Flashes of combat when I'm out of my mind. Screaming. Hysterical. Cutting them down like shooting pop-up clowns at the amusement park.

And there's still lingering memories of Susan. She'll stare at me sometimes. Not with her two blue eyes. But with her one brown eye. That dirty brown eye. That stretched out gaping ass-hole. It stares at me with deceit and lies. And when it stares at me it gets bigger and bigger and bigger. Stretching like some toothless rubbery mouth. Stretching and sucking and consuming. Swallowing that stupid wap with the grease-ball mustache. Swallowing my innocence and my faith. Swallowing my past and my childhood. Swallowing the entire world in her filthy lying ass-eye that stares at me in the dark hours of the never-ending night.

And any chance I get I'm reading Herman Hesse. Thumbing through Demian with the gusto of a kid with his first porn mag. Front to back. Back to front. Searching for meaning. Looking for clues. Reading that one line over and over and over. Deconstructing it word by word. Putting it back together. Hunting for a lead. A symbol. A place to start. Playing bookworm into the early morning hours.

And all the while there's jazz. Always jazz. Filling the room with horns and high-hats. The soundtrack to my thoughts. The oil for my machine mind. Just a rag-tag hotel radio. A beat-up old wooden thing. But it's all I need. And it's always jazz. And it's always smooth and in unison with what I see out my window. The flashing neon alleys. The slow creeping cars. The rain-soaked parking lots. The whole God damned seedy town.

When I'm not locked inside my room banging my head against the wall to the rhythm of the music I'm hanging out with Veronica Vaughn. Killing drizzly afternoons at her apartment. Drinking cheap wine and shooting the shit. Digging one another and making crazy love. Smoking cigarettes in bed. Reading Oscar Wilde out loud at three in the morning. Ripping down all our sexual walls. Exploring. Blossoming. Laughing. Getting stoned and drunk and dancing in her living room to kick-ass jazz tunes cranked up full blast. Taking in shows. Eating Chinese. Going on long romantic walks through the autumn streets. Holding hands. Tickling each other. Giggling. Getting head. Falling in love.

And when I'm not with Veronica I'm out on the city streets. In my Caddy. Cruising here. Rolling there. Keeping a keen eye for anything conspicuous or fishy. Talking to people. Struggling for facts. Meeting strangers and staring in there eyes. Probing there souls for the truth. The truth about them. The truth about this town. The truth about me.

And sometimes I just straight cruise. I hunt. I roll slow like a greasy dream. Crouched low in the seat. Digging it all with mean eyes. By the river where poor black kids play stickball in the mud. Downtown where hustlers and pimps lean against brick walls with their collars up and their gold teeth shinning like a brand new blade. Along the strip where tough-guy dragsters wait at red lights to flex their horse powered muscle machines.

And if I'm not out cruising I'll find myself in a quiet bar sucking down whiskey. I think about my country a lot. That gigantic knock-kneed slut America. Wiggling its patriotic ass for everyone to see. Watching over the world with its atomic eyes. Flashing its switchblade grin at all the commies and savages around the globe. So young. So powerful. So brave. So stupid. Like a swollen man-child with pork chop biceps and T-bone thighs. It regulates the earth with it's hogtie tactics. Stomping around in its steel-toed boots. Making the world safe for democracy.

And sometimes if I look close enough I can see myself in America. I see my sex as the dirty south. The blacks with their railroad shacks and their bayou music. A hot sweaty muddy call for freedom. Something primitive and uninhibited. Jambalaya and voodoo and swamp-rats and chain-gangs and jazz joints and loud fucking and whiskey. It's my sex and I see it as black and down south and dirty.

Where as I see my work ethic as something northern. Something cold and hard and driven. Detroit with its factories and shrill whistles and brutal winters. Downtrodden working class with frozen wills of calloused steel. Driving a pick-up to the warehouse at six in the morning with gloved hands wrapped around a steaming mug of black coffee. That's how I see my work ethic. It puts the food on the table. Period. Paragraph.

But my spirit I see as the west. The wild west. The Oregon trail and the Alamo and Sunset Boulevard and Venice Beach. Baked in sun and hard and vast and macho. Texas cowboys chewing Copenhagen at nine in the morning. Switchblade-toting Zoot Suiters smoking reefer in east L.A.. I see my spirit as wild and massive and untamed.

Truth is I see myself in every part of the country. The redwoods. The ballparks. The wheat fields. The Grand Canyon. The San Francisco bay. The statue of liberty. The graveyards. The hub caps. The highways. The factories. The parades. The sidewalks. The headlines. The poverty. The glamour. The truckers.

The housewives. The tycoons. The pimps. The cops. The pervs. The swing sets. The Oldsmobile's. The handguns. The curling irons.

And then I'll kick back another drink and all my bizarre pathetic ramblings will disappear like a ship pulling out into a foggy harbor.

And this is how things go until one gray and shitty day in mid October. I'm cruising my Cadillac through town just for kicks. Daydreaming. Wasting time. Thinking. Then I pass the public library and a light bulb flashes above my head cartoon style. I can't believe I haven't thought of it sooner. I park my car and head inside.

Same scene as before. Geeks and brainiacs wall to wall. Everybody hard at work. Everybody hush-hush. Everybody getting scoped by the big butch with the barn owl eyes. I make a b-line for the fiction. Check the H's. Still no Hesse. I head up front with my fingers crossed.

"How can I help you" she asks with her glasses still perched on the tip of her nose?

"It's kind of a strange request. I need the name of someone who's got a book checked out."

"I'm afraid I can't give out that information" she says.

"I just thought I'd help the library get its book back" I say spitting spontaneous bullshit.

"What do you mean" she asks?

"I found a copy of Demian in a coffee shop downtown" I say. "It belongs to the library. I would of just returned it myself except I forgot to bring it with me today. And since I don't make it to this part of town very often I thought I'd just give the person a call and tell them I have it."

"I guess we can make an exception" she says. "I'll go get that name for you."

She bought it. Hook line and sinker. A minute later she comes back to the counter. She hands me a small piece of paper.

"The gentleman's name is Gerald Oscar Davidson. I wrote it down for you. And thanks so much for doing this. It's very nice of you."

"Thank yourself darling" I say and give the old lady a wink. "You did all the work."

She blushes an awkward red and turns away. I walk outside smiling on the sly. Smoother than goose shit through a tin horn.

So I have the guy's name. But what am I going to do with it? Is it even a lead? Or is it just a college kid writing a paper on German literature? I have no way of knowing. But my gut tells me I'm onto something. The Hesse connection is too strange to be a coincidence. And there's something vaguely familiar about his name. I repeat it over and over. Nothing clicks.

My mood takes a nosedive. I feel a sudden urge to get incredibly bent. I hit the liquor store and head to my pad with a fat bottle of whiskey.

The place is a wreck. Dirty clothes. Beer bottles. Cigarette butts. God damned pigsty. And the gloomy October light falling through the window doesn't help none. I stand in the doorway looking in. A heavy silence. A feeling of emptiness. A moment of regret and shame. And all because this messy room with the dreary light seems the saddest thing I've ever seen. Then it's gone. Just like that. Like a cloud passing under the sun.

I curl up on the window sill and pour a slug of whiskey in an old paper cup. It burns good and the tear that comes to my eye is like a visit from an old friend. I pour another slug and toss it back. It goes down smooth and easy. The third one goes down the same way. I fire up a Lucky and stare outside.

Evening has moved in. Drizzle falls from the sky. Lightening flashes in the distance. Beat scenes from a hotel window. And down below life plods on like always. A man and woman run to catch the bus. Which I hate to see because there's something so sad and frantic and desperate about people chasing busses. Hipsters in tight jeans and leather jackets loiter on the corner smoking butts and digging the cool October rain. A homeless guy on his hands and knees is sifting through blood at an accident scene looking for loose change. I flick my butt out the window and toss back another shot.

I grab Demian and crawl back onto the window sill to do some reading. Where is the secret? Where is the meaning? Where is the clue that will lead me to the answers I'm looking for? Or do I have it already? Does that one line hold all the answers? Maybe. If only I could understand it. Eventually I grow frustrated. I throw the book across the room and pour a shot of whiskey.

My thoughts turn to Gerald Oscar Davidson. Who is he? Have I met him? And if not why does his name linger so eerily in my mind? Is he a part of all this? Should I contact him? Or just ride it out?

My thoughts are starting to flow smooth from the liquor. It feels as though I might be getting close to something big. But I need a little bit more. I need some reefer. I take a pull from the bottle then start rooting through the room for my stash. When I find it I roll a joint and spark it up. It hits me instantly. I flip on some tunes and fall back onto the bed.

High as hell. Drunk. Eyes closed. Only the music. And the falling falling falling backwards into the abyss of the existential universe. Shreveport Louisiana. Why am I here? Perfectly stoned. Absolutely conscious. Totally dialed in. Because the bird flies to God. Words. Shapes. Ideas. Flashing through my mind like abstract rockets. Because the bird flies to God. And I'm Buckley Finch Wilder. And I'm the bird. No form. No structure. Just straight flowing. Because I'm Buckley Finch Wilder. And I'm the bird. And I fly to God. Flowing like honey. Flowing like jazz. Flowing like semen. But who is God? Jarvis Beauchamp? Ralph Chambers? Gerald Oscar Davidson? Flowing like blood. Flowing like wine. No. No. No. Knuckle-heads and nincompoops. Flowing like Charlie Parker all hopped up on juice dropping crazy improv to an abstract drum beat. Except for maybe Gerald Oscar Davidson. And the grass is setting in for real and I'm getting crazy stoned. And the whiskey is a medicine for a wound I forgot I had. And my mind keeps rolling on like a beat-up jalopy. Hunches. Instincts. Conclusions. Lighting up my skull like a mess of shooting stars. But why? Because the bird flies to God. And my name is Buckley Finch Wilder. And his name is Gerald Oscar Davidson. Stoned to high heaven. Drunk as a skunk. But I'm following the flow because it's leading me somewhere. And I can hear the music in the distance. I think it's King Oliver but I can't tell because I'm so far gone. And all I know is that I'm forever falling backwards into the bed. But it's all coming together. Because his name is Gerald Oscar Davidson. First name Gerald. Middle name Oscar. Last name Davidson. And this is when it all clicks. His fucking initials are G. O. D.. I Buckley Finch Wilder am the Bird and Gerald Oscar Davidson is God and I need to find him. Then I'm swallowed up by a river of booze and smoke. The bed becomes a grave and my mind becomes an aborted baby. I think I hear Lionel Hampton on the radio and then it's darkness and nausea and a whole lot of nothingness.

I wake up a few hours later feeling used up and crusty. The reefer high is splitsville and my liquor buzz is shot to shit. I sit up in bed and fumble for my pack of smokes. I spark a butt and stare zombie-eyed out the window at the lonely night. Beneath the noise of the radio I can hear the pitter-patter of October rain as it falls on the washed-out streets.

There's a sadness in the air. It's in the smell of wet leaves and chimney smoke. It's in the vague sound of ten million strangers shuffling aimlessly along the dark and crooked sidewalks of a faceless America. It's a sweet and gentle sadness. But it's a sadness just the same. I take a deep drag and shut my eyes. And as always when my mind is groggy and vulnerable the memories come creeping in.

Like the way my parent's bodies smelt on the day of their funeral. All bloated and ripe with formaldehyde. I remember the church was dark and eerie. The sound of an organ like some drunken circus nightmare echoed through the halls. I remember opening my Father's coffin lid and grasping for the first time what death really is. A one way door that leads to nowhere. There faces were unrecognizable. Death had taken my parents and twisted them like slabs of clay to resemble things that only exist in the dreams of the demented. And I remember staring down into his broken face until I couldn't take it any longer. I jumped on top of him and held him with all my might. He reeked of chemicals and death but I wouldn't let go. Not until my relatives reached in and pulled me away.

And the years bled together until the war like a thunder cloud moved in and cast its shadow over my soul. The rivers swelled with blood. The screams filled the air. And the ghosts of those we killed roamed among us in the night. Desecrated our dreams. Vandalized our minds. Fucked us while we slept with their decaying dicks and planted the seed of their ruined lives in our hearts to torture us with guilt for the rest of our days.

"Wilder" shouted Sergeant Riggs. "What in the H-E-double hockey stick do you think you're doing? It's two o' clock in the God damned morning. Shouldn't you be in bed cranking your tallywhacker to photos of your old lady?"

"There's something I got to do."

"And what in the name of all that is holy is that" he asked? But just then he saw the body and the shovel and he knew.

"She deserves better" I said.

"She don't deserve shit" he responded. "She's deader than a God damned doornail. And don't go getting all weepy-eyed on me because this gook had shit in her ears. You told her to stop. She didn't. So you can dig her a nice little grave if you want to. You can even get her all gussied up in a pretty gown and slather her fucking face with lipstick if you want to. But that won't change the fact that she's no more alive than a ten pound bag of manure."

"But Sergeant" I said. "She's not a soldier. She's not one of them."

"She is one of them" he screamed. "She's dead. And when you're dead you're not a soldier or a farmer or a mother or nothing. You're maggot feed same as everybody else. Now put her with the rest of the dead and turn in for the night."

"But Sergeant."

"But nothing" he yelled. "I'm the one with the bullshit task of keeping you shit-heels alive. And I don't want anyone out this far at night. Now I'm not asking you Wilder I'm fucking telling you. Leave the bitch where you found her and get your ass back to base."

"With her it was different" I said. "I felt it the second I pulled the trigger. It was wrong. I owe her this."

"If I have to tell you one more God damned time you'll wish your Daddy had pulled out and shot it on the sheet."

"I'm burying her properly" I said.

"The fuck you are."

"The fuck I'm not."

Then he cold-cocked me across the face. I dropped to the dirt. I got up and swung. He dodged it. He threw another punch and I fell to the ground. I got back up. And so began a dark and ugly war of wills. He was too tough to beat and I was too stupid to give up. He kept knocking me down and I kept getting back up. Over and over until my face looked like a plate of spaghetti.

"You better beat me to death" I shouted with a mouthful of blood. "Because if you leave me standing I'm going to fucking bury her."

"Go ahead and bury the stupid bitch" he screamed. "Bury yourself while you're at it. I'm starting to think you cock-suckers are made for each other."

Then he walloped me again. Hard as hell. I spun around and crumbled to the ground. When I opened my eyes he was gone. The rain had started. I was all alone. I pulled myself through the mud toward the old woman. When I reached her I collapsed. My head rested on her Swiss cheese chest. I began to sob. And the blood and the tears and the rain became as one. It tasted like flat beer. And all was safe for democracy.

I take another deep drag and let my thoughts drift toward the present. To the city of Shreveport. To my bizarre and wonderful life with Veronica Vaughn. To memories of earlier that day. The library. The name. The liquor. The dope. The epiphany I received in the midst of my wasted stupor. And then it all comes rushing back. Everything is clear again. Everything makes sense.

I grab a beat-up old phone book from the bedside drawer and open it to the D's. There it is. Gerald Oscar Davidson. 117 Maple Lane. I grind the butt in the ashtray and rise to face the night.

A shower and a shave and I'm feeling like the cat's pajamas. I get directions to Maple Lane at a gas station near my pad then I swing by the Blue Room to say hi to Veronica.

I pull up out front and toss the keys to the fresh-faced kid working valet. The monkey watching the door opens it up and steps aside. They've been treating me like a celebrity since they found out I'm dating Veronica. Same service inside. Smiles form the staff. Handshakes from the manager. I park it at an empty stool and the bartender is quick to light my smoke.

"What do you say Buckley" he asks?

"Any cheap and tawdry thing that'll get me a beer" I respond.

"Coming right up" he chuckles as he spins around and starts pouring.

When he's done I toss him some cash and slip backstage to find Veronica. Her door is unlocked. I let myself in. She's sitting in a chair facing he door. She's smoking a cigarette. Her hair is perfect. Her makeup is stunning. Her evening gown shows lots of leg and ample cleavage. She's dynamite from head to toe.

"What's going on Veronica" I ask?

"Let's talk about what's going in Veronica" she replies.

"If I didn't know any better I'd think you just suggested a quickie."

"The quicker the better" she says setting her cigarette in the ashtray. "I'm back on stage in five minutes."

I toss back the rest of my beer I watch her slip her panties off. She spreads her legs seductively and the snatch shot I get is an open invitation to take what I see and do with it as I please. I set my glass down and move toward her. She has my pants around my ankles quicker than I can say button fly. I pick her up. She wraps her legs around my waist. I pin her against the wall. I feel my cock slip inside.

She has a pussy like a velvet bear trap. Tight and smooth. And when it clamps down on me I'd sell my soul to make the pleasure last just a few seconds longer. Making love to Veronica is like eating at my favorite restaurant. I always know what I'm going to get and I always leave with a smile on my face.

I really start hammering it. I squeeze her ass cheeks and pull her up and down the length of my cock. The pace is frantic. Her nails are digging into my back. Her breath is hot on my neck. My biceps are burning. Sweat is dripping from my forehead. But I keep at it. And soon we're both screaming nasty stuff and everything is bright and tingly and happy and sexy.

Afterwards Veronica picks up her cigarette from the ashtray. It's still burning. She takes a drag then grabs her panties from the floor and steps into them.

"And to what do I owe this surprise visit" she asks as she fixes her hair in the mirror?

"I was on my way to find G.O.D. and I just thought I'd stop in and say hi."

"It's about time you straightened your act up" she says with a smile. "But you might have a hard time finding a church open at ten o' clock on a Tuesday night."

"I plan on catching him at home" I say. "I know where he lives."

"Really" she asks? "And where's that?"

"117 Maple Lane."

"All right wise guy" she says turning to face me. "I give up. What gives?"

"I think I figured out what that Herman Hesse passage is all about. There's a fellow in town named Gerald Oscar Davidson. I think I need to meet him."

"I didn't think you were actually going religious on me" she says.

"Making love to you is the only religious experience I need."

"Why don't you swing by my place later tonight" she says. "And we'll have another religious experience."

"Hallelujah" I say with a smirk and a wink.

"Now kiss me quick you big lug" she says. "I'm late for the stage."

So I do. Then she rubs her cigarette out in the ashtray and heads for the door.

"Buckley" she says turning to face me. "Be careful."

"I'll see you tonight" I say as I ogle her sweet can swaying out the door.

By the time I leave the club the night is darker than a well digger's asshole. No moon. No stars. Just the black clouds covering the whole God damned city like a coffin lid. And down in the meat of the earth we humans scurry aimlessly through the maze like pale bugs beneath a sheet of plywood that's been lying in the yard too long.

Skid row drifters in dead end alleys cook hot dogs on coat hangers over trash barrel fires. Drunken floozies in broken heels wobble home after a long night of unsuccessful flirting. A stray dog with a crooked tail and a scabby eye roams the streets looking for handouts that it'll never get.

Soon I'm out of downtown and entering a swanky neighborhood. Streets lined with massive trees. Beautiful yards. Ritzy homes. Driveways full of cherry rides.

I hit Maple Lane and hang a right. The homes get even nicer. I imagine the owners to be lawyers and judges and investment tycoons. I envision them sitting in their wood-paneled studies smoking fancy cigars and drinking fifty year old whiskey out of crystal tumblers. And their wives who are all one time prom queens wear polka dot aprons and bake cherry pies while listening to Gershwin on the radio. It's the world of the elite and the privileged. A world most folks never see save for visits to the silver screen.

Maple Lane begins sloping gently upwards and when I reach the crest of the small hill I look to my left and see it. It's the sweetest pad on the whole block. It's a Victorian style number. Overwhelming in size. Immaculate in detail.

There's no lights on and there's no cars in the driveway so I assume the place is empty. At the risk of getting the fuzz called on me I decide to have a look inside.

I park my car around the corner and grab a flashlight out of the glove box. When I reach the house I listen for sounds and when I'm confident the place is empty I sneak around back and try one of the windows. It's unlocked. I crawl inside.

I find myself standing in a kitchen the size of a God damned ball park. But what the room possesses in size and opulence it lacks in tidiness. Dishes are heaped high on the counter. A trashcan is filled to the rim. Empty booze bottles are scattered across the room. I tiptoe out of the kitchen and down a hallway.

I enter a large room. It's cozy and appears well lived in. An enormous rug covers most of the hardwood floor. It's maroon and gold and intricately woven. On the far wall is a fire place with a massive wooden mantle. There's a couple of sofas. Some reading chairs. A coffee table. A floor lamp.

I creep further into the room. Strange details are revealed. Beer bottles. Candy wrappers. Dirty ashtrays. The room is nothing but a den of gross self-indulgence. A portrait of wealth gone awry. Riches turned sour. And as I look around the room at all the decadence and misguided privilege I can't tell if what I feel is envy or disgust.

I leave the room and cut back down the hallway. I pass the kitchen and come to a massive foyer. There's a chandelier hanging from the ceiling. An ornamental staircase. A huge front door flanked by stained glass windows. To the left of the stairs is a door. I open it up and look in. The stairs go down.

I head down the stairs into the basement. Slowly. Quietly. Methodically. I let my hand slide along the banister and it calls up images of my childhood when I viewed stairs as a symbol of financial stability. The more stairs the greater the wealth. I find it fitting that this memory comes to me while descending the stairs of a home I have just broken into. The years slip by and not much really changes. Those who got it flaunt it. And those without a buck are shit out of luck.

At the bottom of the stairs I turn right and walk to the end of the hallway where a door stands slightly ajar. I push it open. It's an office. I step inside and start snooping around. The sidewalls are book shelves floor to ceiling. The wall in front of me has a ground level window facing the backyard. Below the window sits an enormous mahogany desk. On the desk is a beat-up typewriter. Next to the typewriter is a stack of books. I scan the tittles. They're all Herman Hesse novels. I grab Demian from the pile and flip it open. Some lines have been highlighted with a red marker. "Who would be born must first destroy a world. The bird flies to God." I set the book down and start rummaging through the desk.

The top drawer is full of photographs. I pick one up. It's of the Korean woman I killed. She's dressed like a bum and has a patch over one eye. She's kneeling on the sidewalk. She's all beat and sad looking. She's holding an old tin cup and a cardboard sign with the words "hungry please help." On the back is written "NYC 1948."

The next photo is of Veronica Vaughn. She's standing behind the counter of some greasy spoon. Outside the window I can make out a busy intersection flooded with cabs and huge buildings rising up into the sky. She's wearing a hat and a nametag. She's a waitress. She's just standing there looking all forlorn and dejected. On the back is written "NYC 1949."

The next photo is of my Mom and Dad. They're standing on the sidewalk in front of a shoe repair shop. Dad is resting an elbow on the sign and Mom has her arm around him. They have big jovial grins and humble eyes. They appear healthy and proud and happy to be there. The back of the photo reads "The We've Got Sole Shoe Repair Shop. 1945."

The next photo is of me. I'm wearing a mud stained football uniform with the number 43 on the front. I'm kneeling in the center of a field holding a ball. There's a whole mess of players and parents standing around staring at me with bright faces and outstretched arms. The back reads "Conference Championship Game. East Shreveport 37 Jefferson 21."

The next photo is of me again. It's graduation day. I'm standing out front of a high school. I'm wearing the typical robe and ugly hat. I have my arms around two guys. We're all smiling and laughing and hanging onto one another. It reads "High School Graduation. 1938."

I keep flipping through the photos and they're all of me or of people I know. My entire history is here. But it's all fucked up. Backwards. Twisted. Rearranged. It's as if my life is a jigsaw puzzle that has been taken apart and put back in the box and shaken up until nothing makes sense. Right people wrong place. Right place wrong time. None of the pieces fit together. And the more I try the more I feel my brain bend in ways it's not meant to bend. I decide to call it quits for the night. I put the photos back in the desk and blow the fucking joint.

I drive like an animal until I see some Ma and Pa mart sitting on the corner of two deadbeat streets. The rain is falling like teardrops through the midnight sky and the neon sign is tossing its dirty red glow onto the gravel like a bucket of rotten blood. I buy a twelve pack of Miller and a pack of Lucky Strikes then sit in the parking lot and chug two cans to my head. It's enough to take the edge off and I pull out onto the road with a full head of steam and a mind as twisted bag full of intestines.

I cruise the dark highways along the outskirts of town. I play the radio loud. I sing along. And when my thoughts turn dark and menacing I crouch low in the seat and chug another beer then toss it out the window and listen as the can bounces along the black-top making that lonely tinkle sound like a pathetic wind-chime hanging from the eaves of an old widow's trailer. The autumn air is cool and feels like some kind of heaven whipping in all fresh across my face. I smoke my Lucky down to the butt and flick it out the window then check the mirror real quick to see the little red sparks tumbling over the sad asphalt darkness.

And when the beer runs out I don't stop. I find some old roadside tavern and take my place at the bar with all the other piss-ants and losers and social retards. There's an over the hill hooker from Cheyenne with makeup like a layer of tasteless wallpaper who's on her way to Florida to find some trick who broke her heart in the late nineteen thirties. There's a world war one vet with a missing leg and a voice like a tin cup full of gravel who spends his nights drinking cheap wine and blubbering about the throats he slit while fighting in the trenches of Germany. There's an aging conman who with his million dollar smile and razor-thin mustache still can't hide his snake in the grass eyes. And he sits there doing card tricks and not caring that nobody watches just so long as his gold rings twinkle pretty in the light as his pudgy little fingers work the cards. There's a thirty-something housewife with a black eye the size of a hubcap and nobody knows if she's drinking to drown the shame of being some grease-ball's punching bag or if she's building up the courage to slit the fucker's throat in the middle of the night while he sleeps. There's some wet behind the ears college kid who probably hasn't shaved a day in his life and looks as out of place as a two dollar whore at Sunday morning service but nobody flicks him any shit because at least he's out looking for something other than a white picket fence and a nine to five job sucking dick for the man.

And everybody is real. And everybody is thirsty. And everybody lines up against the altar to get lit up like a Christmas tree. Because there's a tragic beauty that can only be found in the dregs of societies filth. But you're not going to stumble upon it by chance. You have to work for it. You have to get on your hands and knees like a starving bum and dig. You have to scratch at the clay and mud until your fingernails crack and bleed. You have to crawl through the shit and the vomit and the jizz. And if you find it be careful because it's a slippery son of a bitch and it's easy to lose.

But we find it at the tavern. And we hold onto it tight. We spit on it and shine it up all pretty. We hold it up in the air like a severed head and sound the call of the ravenous masses.

And when closing time comes I'm not done so I talk the bartender into pouring my beer into a paper cup and I say good-bye to the people of the abyss then take off into the night.

I'm a bird of prey. I fly fast and deadly over the immaculate earth. Past barns and tractors and cornfields and scarecrows. Past billboards and gas stations and truck stops and diners. And I play the radio loud. And I scream at the clouds. And I curse at the darkness.

And when I hit downtown I'm still not done so I shoot over to Veronica's and stumble up stairs. I put on a Ella Fitzgerald record and rip the blankets off her bed and when I see her pink naked body squirming in the sheets I jump her bones and behave like a pig. And not a sweet fat jovial pig that gives rides to the farm kids but a mean old pig that's starving and half-mad and ornery as hell.

And I fuck her filthy and I fuck her hard and I fuck her to forget about everything that's wrong with my God damned life. To forget about Korea. To forget about my folks. And most of all to forget about those photos. But my mind is like a strip of flypaper and these memories are stuck for good. And so I just keep fucking her until I blow my wad then roll over and lie there smoking and staring up into nothing while the weight of my thoughts crush me like a peanut shell under the boot of a beer-bellied trucker.

CHAPTER 8

▼

A HANGOVER AN EMPTY GAS TANK AND A SORE COCK

We're sitting in a booth at a trendy little breakfast joint around the corner from Veronica's. The name is The Playground and the owner is a three hundred pound bald fruitcake named Ricky who wears bright tweed suits and flashy silk scarves and has a mustache like a squirrel's tail. Ricky not only owns the place but hosts and waits tables as well and watching him perform all three tasks at once offers as much entertainment as we're likely to find in Shreveport at eleven in the morning. It keeps things light and gives us a quick out if conversation gets too deep. Which it does in no time flat.

"Don't go back there" Veronica begs. "Please don't go back there."

"I have to."

"Why" she asks?

"What do you mean why? I told you what I saw. Doesn't it strike you a bit strange that there's a picture of you in New York when you've never actually been there? And what about me? There's a picture of me playing football for Christ's sake. I never played football in my whole God damned life."

"Can't you just forget about the photos" she asks? "Can't we just leave and start a new life together somewhere else and pretend you never saw them?"

"Believe me I tried" I say. "I spent all last night trying to forget what I saw. It doesn't work. All I got is a hangover an empty gas tank and a sore cock."

"Listen buster" she says. "I'm the one who could hardly walk this morning. I didn't know if you were making love to me or trying to pin me."

"I'm sorry" I say. "But that's just what I'm talking about. I don't want to spend the rest of my life pouring liquor down my throat and acting like an animal just to get some peace of mind. If I don't face this thing now it could wreck us both forever."

"But aren't you worried Buckley" she asks? "Aren't you scared?"

"You're God damned right I'm scared."

Enter Ricky . Right on cue. Flustered and agitated and making a scene. His bald head is shiny with sweat. His three chins are quivering. One hand rests on his hip. The other holds a piece of asparagus. He waves it threateningly at the kitchen staff. Two Mexican guys and a high school boy.

"Why are you overcooking the asparagus" he asks? "Do you guys have any idea how much I pay for this stuff? It's obscene. The produce guy's got me the balls. Which wouldn't be so bad if he didn't look like Boris Karlof."

Then he storms off with his nose in the air and his little scarf billowing behind him. And nobody knows if they should cry or laugh or applaud the performance. But in the end it doesn't matter. They all leave smiling. They all come back. And big Ricky is always here to greet them.

"I'm going with you then" she demands.

"Going with me where?"

"Tonight" she says sipping her coffee. "I'm going with you tonight. Back to that house."

"The hell you are" I say. "This is my problem. Not yours."

"What do you mean it's not my problem? I'm in the photos just like you."

"Listen" I say trying to keep my cool. "I don't want you getting anymore involved. I got us in this mess and I'm going to get us out."

"But" she says.

"But nothing Veronica."

Then there's a loud crash as a tray of dirty dishes hits the floor. Ricky's timing is impeccable. He dances nervously around the mess. His face a bright blushing red. His pudgy fingers pulling frantically at his mustache.

"Well doesn't that just suck the big one" he says as he undoes his scarf and dabs at the sweat on his forehead.

We never resume our conversation. We drink coffee and laugh and try not to think about what the night holds in store. And when we leave the diner Ricky waves his scarf and blows us a kiss and we stumble out onto the sidewalk giggling and blissful and in love.

From then on the day assumes a dreamlike quality. Whimsical. Directionless. It feels like one of those dates when you don't know whether you're ever going to see each other again after it ends. And so you don't think about it. You just keep playing and smiling and being thankful for every moment you have together.

Happy and free we stroll hand in hand through the misty autumn streets. We kiss in the park and run through piles of golden yellow leaves. We have ice cream for lunch and have martinis for dessert. We dance on the sidewalk and run through the streets. We shop. We play. We flirt. We fall in love all over again. And when the rain comes we duck inside a theatre and catch a matinee of an old western film. We have popcorn and soda and laugh and make-out. And after the show we take a drive in my Caddy out to the country where we park and watch the sun set slow and golden on the river.

We crawl in the back. And with the sky on fire and the radio playing softly we have sweet sex and forget about everything other than each other and the love we share. We fall asleep in the back seat of my car. All twisted up together like a pile of driftwood.

But sleep doesn't take your problems away. It just hides them for a while. And eventually we wake up to the grim realization that it's eight-thirty at night and time for me to get going.

We drive in silence all the way back to Veronica's place. I pull up out front and kill the engine. We sit there for a while without saying anything. We don't even look at each other. Eventually Veronica breaks the silence.

"Just because I can't change your mind doesn't mean I have to be happy about it."

"I'm not happy about it either" I say. "But I promised myself I was going to follow this thing through to the end and that's what I'm going to do."

I don't allow her to respond. Instead I just lean over and plant a wet one on her cheek then open the door and say good-night. She kisses me again then steps out onto the curb. I watch her in my rearview mirror as I drive away. She's still standing there as I round the corner and disappear into the night.

I'm at my pad in no time flat. I take a hot shower then go back to my room. I get dressed then grab the gun and head out the door.

The streets are deadsville and I make it to his house in a flash. This time somebody's home. A brand new white Buick is parked in the driveway and some lights are on inside. I park out front and stick the gun in my belt. I get out of the car and when I'm sure nobody's looking I head toward the house.

I creep around back and that's when I first see him. There's a light coming from the window of the basement study. I crouch beside the house and peer in. He's sitting at the desk. He's hunched over the typewriter pecking at the keys like a buzzard cleaning the meat off a greasy rib bone.

He stops typing to look at what he's written and that's when I see his face. He's a frail man. Around the age of thirty. He has fair skin. His hair is blonde and combed tightly back. His mustache is well-groomed but appears unnatural because it doesn't match his hair color. It looks as if someone has drawn it on with a marker. He's wearing a red silk robe with a dragon on the front and is smoking some fancy little cigarette.

Looking pleased with what he has written he settles back into his chair and begins typing again. I watch him type and as I do I begin to experience a crazy sensation. It feels as though he knows I'm watching him. As if he has not only been expecting me but has actually orchestrated the entire thing. Finally the feeling gets too strong and I race around to the front of the house to confront him.

The door opens after the second knock. The man sticks his head out.

"Are you Gerald Oscar Davidson" I ask?

"Yes" he replies. "What can I do for you?"

"You can start talking" I say as I draw my gun and push open the door. "I need some fucking answers."

"Well" he says as he turns and walks down the hallway. "I've really outdone myself. You're a genuine tough guy. A true ruffian."

He enters the living room and I follow him with my gun aimed at his back. He makes his way to the fireplace and grabs a bottle of bourbon from off the mantle. After finding an empty paper cup on the ground he pours a generous slug and sits down on the couch.

"Care to join me for a cocktail" he asks holding up the bottle of liquor? "I'll even get you a glass. None of this paper shit for the guest of honor."

"I didn't come here to make a new drinking buddy. I came here for some answers."

"Oh lighten up" he says. "I know why you're here. Hell I've been expecting you."

He downs the cup of whiskey and pours himself another. He downs that one as quick as the first then fumbles in his robe for a pack of Pall Malls. He lights one then leans back in the couch and crosses his legs like a woman. I watch him closely. Size him up. Scrutinize his every move. I feel a strong dislike toward him. He strikes me as a fellow in dire need of a good old fashioned ass whooping.

"Explain the photos in your desk downstairs" I demand.

"What about them" he asks?

"Who's the sexy dame waiting tables?"

"I don't know her name" he says. "If that's what you mean. She's just a hot broad who used to wait on me at a diner in New York. I liked her tits so I took a photograph of her."

"Watch your mouth wise guy" I say. "That's my girl you're talking about"

"I love it when you talk like that" he says with a disturbing little giggle. "You really are a perfect tough guy. Absolutely perfect."

"What about the one with the old couple in front of the shoe shop" I ask? "Are you going to tell me that they're not my parents?"

"Those aren't your parents" he says mockingly. "They're just an old couple from New York."

"You're full of shit" I yell. "And what about the pictures of me? Who the fuck is that?"

"It's my younger brother" he says softly as he pours another shot of whiskey. "Fucking drunk driver killed him when he was only eighteen."

"That's me in the photograph" I holler. "And you know it. Now tell me what the fuck's going on around here."

"Where's the fun in that? Besides" he chuckles as he drinks his whiskey. "You've made it this far you deserve to uncover the truth by yourself."

"Then tell me where I can find it" I ask?

"Right here of course. In my house. Go ahead and look. Turn the place upside down. I want you to find it."

"Have it your way" I say as I turn and leave the room.

I trash the joint. I start in the upstairs bedroom and work my way down. Tipping furniture. Pulling out drawers. Digging through paper work. Rummaging through closets. Knocking shelves over. And the whole time I can hear him down in the living room laughing and drinking and acting like it's a big fucking joke. This only makes me more angry. I tear through the upstairs like a whirlwind of hate and destruction.

"You're getting hotter" he yells as I come down the stairs.

I enter the living room and the site of him sitting there with a bottle of whiskey and a shit-eating grin on his face makes me completely lose it. I start going wild. Crazy. Cussing. Mumbling. Kicking over tables. Ripping apart pillows. Smashing. Shattering. Crushing. Tearing. When I'm done in the living room I stumble into the hall.

"You're almost on fire" he yells with amusement as I approach the basement door. "You're burning up."

I know I'm getting close. I slam open the door and rush down the stairs into the basement. I head straight for the study and start ransacking the joint top to bottom. I look in all the desk drawers. I dig through the closet. I even rip up the carpet. Then I knock a painting off the wall and that's when I see it. A small compartment set in the wall. A stash box.

I turn the handle and the metal door opens smoothly. My eyes bulge and my knees threaten to buckle. Inside the wall is the briefcase. Also in the stash box is a key. I grab both items and set them on the desk.

With the eerie sound of Gerald Oscar Davidson cackling in the background I insert the key and slowly open the briefcase. Inside is a stack of papers. A manuscript. Suddenly my thoughts are like a merry-go-round spinning out of control and my mind is a third grader clinging pathetically to the bars trying not to get thrown off into the mud. With trembling hands I pick it up and begin to read.

Fresh out of the corps and already my life is mangled beyond all recognition. In Korea on those long sweaty nights when the mountains threaten to swallow me whole and shit out my bones in the shape of a grave I dream about the states. But now that I'm back I already miss the simplicity of combat. A group of men I can trust my life with and an enemy who opposes my existence. It's easy. It makes sense. I don't have to think. But back in the states it's nothing but thinking. It's all one big puzzle and I'm the piece that doesn't seem to fit right.

I drop the papers on the floor and take a seat. I kick my feet up on the desk and fire up a Lucky Strike. I inhale the smoke good and deep. I close my eyes and recline back in the chair. It's a struggle to keep my thoughts in order. In fact it's useless. Uncountable epiphanies are occurring simultaneously. The entire framework of my mind is crashing down. And out of the rubble a new structure comes lurching upward. A metamorphosis is underway. My head threatens to crack from the tension. And just when I think my skull can endure no more the transformation comes to a sudden halt.

"Holly shit" I say as I open my eyes and blow out a mouthful of smoke. "I'm fucking fiction."

CHAPTER 9

▼

IT ENDS WITH YOU
WALKING OUT THAT FRONT
DOOR

He's still sitting on the couch as I stroll forlornly into the living room. He's still dolled up in that ridiculous red robe. He's still holding the bottle of whiskey. He's still wearing that shit-eating grin. I sit down in a chair and put my feet up on the coffee table. His gaze makes me feel uneasy. It's condescending. Pompous. Proud. Like some smug artist admiring his own work. I whip out another Lucky and light up.

"Are you sure you don't want a beverage" he asks?

"You tell me" I say considering what I've just discovered. "Do I?"

"Yes" he says pouring a shot of whiskey into a cup. "You do."

"Thanks" and I reach out and take the cup from his hand.

Then we sit for a moment in silence. I smoke. I drink my whiskey. I let my thoughts take shape. There's so much I want to ask. So much I still need to know. But does it even matter anymore? Does anything matter now?

"You weren't lying about those photographs were you" I ask?

"No" he moans. "I wasn't."

"So everybody I've ever met is just people from your life?"

"Why invent characters when you can borrow from reality" he asks sitting up and rubbing at his bloodshot eyes? "It's more believable. More authentic."

"How did you end up in New York" I ask?

"The real question" he says. "Is how did I end up back here? Growing up all I thought about was getting out of this pathetic town. That's why I moved to New York in the first place. I went to school at Columbia. Graduated four years later with a degree in English literature. Since then I've just been playing in the city and living off my allowance. Then my father goes and dies of a heart attack and I have to come back here and take care of all his shit. As if he wasn't satisfied controlling my life while he was alive he has to go and pull a stunt like this. It's fucking typical. Piece of shit. I came back to Shreveport about six months ago and that's when I decided to start working on my novel. Might as well. I'm just killing time waiting for the home to sell. Living off my father's investments. That's one thing I will say for the fat old fucker. I have always enjoyed spending his money."

He leans back into the couch. Exhausted. As if the telling of his story has stripped his energy clean. He closes his eyes and seems to shrink into himself. To recede. To shrivel up. I grind my cigarette in the ashtray and pour another cup of liquor.

I think once again about the pictures. About all the people I met during my life. The family. The friends. The broads. The guys who fought beside me in Korea. They're all just cardboard cutouts and don't even know it. Ignorant pawns marching mindlessly across a world that doesn't exist. How could a secret so massive been kept for so long? How can someone as unworthy as Gerald Oscar Davidson control the fate of so many? What gives him the right to keep us blind and stupid? What gives him the right to play God?

"How could you" I demand?

"How could I what" he asks with his eyes opening slowly.

"How could you do this to all of us? These are real people you know. With real lives and real identities. It may not seem that way to you. But it's true. In their own way they're real."

He sits up and lights a Pall Mall. He inhales it deep and the smoke seems to bring him back to life. His eyes open wide. Too wide. They're like bloodshot hubcaps spinning down the highway. All crazy and wild and twirly. He's reached that scary drunk when the booze is too big for his body and his skin wants to rip open and let it all out.

"Have you ever heard the saying 'don't bite the hand that feeds you'" he asks? "With out me you wouldn't have a pot to shit in. None of you would even exist.

So don't whine to me about real people. I know you're real. Hell I created all of you. I can do whatever I God dammed want."

"Just because you can do something doesn't make it right" I say. "What about all these people who think they actually exist? What happens when they find out they don't? What then?"

"They won't" he says with a mouthful of smoke.

"Why not" I ask? "I did."

"You only found out because I wanted you to find out. That's the way I wrote it. That's what the fucking book is about. About a guy who realizes he doesn't exist."

"Then what about the others" I ask?

"What others? You're the only one who knows."

"That's not true" I say. "What about Jarvis Beauchamp? He knows. And his friend Ralph Chambers is not far behind. What about them?"

"They don't know shit" he says. "Never have. Jarvis is just a short story that I wrote a few years ago. I just put him in as a clue."

"What are you talking about?"

"I came up with him back in New York" he says and blows a couple of smoke rings into the air. "I wrote a short story about a man who only spoke with book quotes. The story turned out to be shit. But I liked the idea. And so I decided to use his character in this novel. Problem is when I originally wrote the story I had him quoting James Joyce. It didn't work with this book. I needed a passage that served as a clue. Something that would lead you to me. And so I started brain-storming. Researching. Because of my initials I wanted to find a passage that said something about God. That's when I remembered Herman Hesse. I picked up a few of his books and that's when I found it. 'Who would be born must first destroy a world. The bird flies to God.' All I had to do was give you the middle name Finch and it made perfect sense. Not that that's as easy as it sounds. You try coming up with a bird name that still sounds macho. You're lucky your name isn't Buckley Hummingbird Wilder."

He falls back into the couch and laughs hysterically. He looks like a frightened rat. His teeth long and skinny. His lips pulled back tight. His thin mustache twitching like whiskers. I sip my beverage and turn my gaze elsewhere.

"Well that explains it" I say when his laughter finally stops.

"Explains what?"

"Why all the Hesse books were checked out at the library. And here I thought you were just some putz like me. Some schmuck following the same lead I was. But I do have one question."

"What" he asks?

"How did I talk to the librarian if I'm not real?"

"Jesus Christ" he says. "Don't you get it? That wasn't a real librarian. Nobody you've ever spoken with has been real. You're entire life has been fiction. Even this right now is just a chapter in the book. Everything you've excepted as real comes to an end right now. Your life as you know it is over."

Once again he starts cackling like a madman. Once again he resembles a hissing rodent. Once again I have to avert my gaze and fight the urge to slap the condescension off his face. But even the sound of his laughter is enraging. It bores into my ears like an old rusty drill bit. I finish my whiskey and throw the cup on the floor. I wait for him to get a grip on himself. When he does I press on.

"And the briefcase" I ask?

"What about it?"

"Who stole it from me?"

"Nobody" he says. "You never had it. At least not the real one. I've had the real one the entire time. I use it to store my manuscript in."

"OK smart guy" I say. "Let me rephrase that. Who stole the fictional briefcase from me?"

"The same person who gave it to you" he says.

"The old guy? That's impossible. I saw him die."

"Not him" he says. "Me. I'm the author remember. I put the briefcase in your possession. And I took it away from you too."

"But how" I demand?

"What do you mean how? I just did it. I sat at my typewriter and did it. I erased it. I removed it from your trunk."

"That's cheating" I say. "You can't just do that. You should at least have a character from the novel steal it from me."

"I did" he answers with a smirk and puts his cigarette out in the ashtray. "I am a character. I wrote myself into my own novel."

I shake my head in frustration. There's no way out. Nowhere left to go. Not only am I fiction but the author is a fucking prick. I'm just a puppet on a string. A play toy. A soulless zombie imprisoned in some trashy pulp novel. A one-dimensional tough guy for the boys to admire and the dames to get off on.

"So what now" I ask feeling exhausted and confused?

"Now I finish writing my novel."

"I know" I say. "But what happens next?"

"I don't know" he sighs. "This chapter's as far as I've made it."

"And how does this chapter end" I ask?

"It ends with you walking out that front door."

I stand up. My legs feel heavy and stiff. Like two slabs of concrete. I pull out my pack of Lucky Strikes and light one up. The smoke tastes good. I hold it in for a long time. Then I nod my head at Gerald Oscar Davidson and walk out of the room.

When I reach the front door I pause for a moment to gather my courage. I step outside. Out into the desolate fall night. Out into the great unknown. Out into the barren void of my new world. Out into the jaws of oblivion itself.

PART II

CHAPTER 10

▼

A PERFECT AND
MEANINGLESS ETERNITY

Is consciousness something you are given like a name or a birth certificate? Can you buy it at the corner market along with your hair tonic and your condoms? Or is it something you've got to earn through hard work and sweat? What does it mean to be alive? What is the nature of existence? Is reality set in stone? Or is it just some filthy poem scribbled on the inside of a restroom stall? Always changing. Always evolving. Always awaiting the next juvenile vandal to carve their own contribution.

I remember as a kid lying on the back porch staring up at the stars pretending that the whole world was really just a shack I had made out of scrap wood and that the stars were just nail holes where the light from some great and unknown reality came seeping through. I remember wringing my mind like a soggy washcloth trying to fathom what might be out there causing all that light. I remember growing up and reading books under the covers at night by flashlight hoping to stretch the boundaries of my mind so that someday I could put the whole puzzle together.

I know now that these memories never actually happened. But does that make them any less real? Aren't all memories fabrications to a certain degree? Lumps of shit that we've polished so thoroughly over the years that they come to resemble sparkling diamonds. And what about my need for understanding? It isn't some switch I can flick on and off with my finger. Not some cheap broad that I keep on standby and only call when I'm desperate and horny. But where am I supposed to go? How can I continue on? What can I do now that I've found out I'm just some asshole's brainchild?

It shouldn't matter really. Aren't we all creations? Aren't we all squirted out of the universal vagina? Thrust into existence like a child tossed into a river by a sink or swim Father? Maybe I'm just bitter about slipping down the totem pole of creation. Bumped from varsity to the JV squad.

Or maybe it's regret at having met my maker face to face. At having all my notions of an all-powerful creator shattered like a mouthful of butterbrickle. What would of happened if Moses hadn't seen the burning bush and instead found some cross-eyed drunk with blisters on his lips rubbing his dick in the sand? What if Paul instead of a blinding light was confronted by a contortionist with his head stuck in his ass? What would people think if they found out their God was just a panty-sniffing pervert with three nipples and two assholes and the nasty habit of drinking his own vomit? Who knows? Who cares? It isn't they who have to wander along dragging this burden like a splintery cross. It's me.

It isn't easy getting used to. In fact it's a total drag. Everything I have ever known to be real is flushed down the crapper in a big bloody clump. I'm forced to start from scratch. I have to build myself from the ground up. I have to begin again.

At first I hardly get out of bed. It's not that I choose not to. It's that I choose not to choose at all. I wait for something to pull me off the mattress. Some force to guide me here or there. But it never comes. And so I just keep lying here.

I'm completely indifferent to the whole thing. I don't give a rat's ass one way or the other. I stare out the window with a cold and empty mind. Confused. Lonely. Stiff as a corpse. I count the cracks that run across the ceiling. I watch the shadows grow long and dark. Then I watch them shrink back as the lights come on at night. The rain taps at the window with a million wet fingers. The wind howls with a mouth made out of clouds. The naked branches point in at me accusingly.

Boredom sets in. Followed by depression. Hygiene is neglected entirely. My hair turns greasy. A beard appears upon my face. Rancid breath. Body odor. Bed soars. Fingernails like yellow snail shells. I begin to fall apart. I feel myself deteriorating. I feel myself dying. But I don't fight it. I embrace it. I cuddle it like a worn-out teddy bear.

And then one day it happens. I grow tired of waiting. I grow bored of being bored. I don't view it as a personal victory. I don't credit myself. I just assume that Gerald Oscar Davidson has finally decided what to do with the story. And so I go with the flow. I get dressed and stumble out into the midday streets.

It's early December and people with umbrellas and overcoats hurry along the crowded sidewalks. Those caught unprepared hold newspapers over their heads or scamper from awning to awning like rats trying to avoid being seen.

I stroll right down the middle of the sidewalk with my arms stretched out in a scarecrow pose letting the rain soak my beard and fill my eyes. People look at me with pity and scorn. I pay no attention. Anyone who sees me doesn't exist anyways. So fuck them.

I spend the entire afternoon walking in the rain. Through the park. Along the sidewalks. Under the bridges. Like a grocery bag blown by the wind. Directionless and free. Many thoughts pass through my mind. But most of which are of Veronica Vaughn. I miss her like crazy. I want to see her. But what would I tell her? How would I explain my absence? The truth? Would she buy it if I told her? Would she even want to know? I have no idea. But I have to find out. I have to assume that our love is worth fighting for. I walk to my Cadillac and drive out to her place.

"You asshole" she screams from the bedroom as I enter her apartment. "I thought you were dead. You better have a fucking good explanation. You can't just disappear like that and then come crawling back to me out of the blue."

But the screaming stops when I enter the bedroom dripping rainwater and looking like hell. Her jaw drops. Her eyes get huge with concern. She clumsily puts her cigarette out in the ashtray and runs to my embrace.

"Jesus Christ Buckley. What happened?"

"Veronica" I say holding her tight. "There's something I got to tell you. And it's not going to be easy."

"Where have you been" she asks? "I haven't seen you in over a month."

"I've suffered a bit of a breakdown."

"Join the club you prick" she says fighting back the tears. "I thought I had lost you for good."

"Well I'm still here. Kind of."

"What do you mean kind of" she asks? "Where have you been?"

"It's not that easy" I say. "It's complicated."

"I don't care. I want to know where the hell you've been."

"I'll tell you if you just let me pull myself together."

"Pull my ass" she screams. "I want to know where the fuck you've been."

"Listen" I yell taking her by the shoulders and shaking her. "We don't fucking exist."

What follows is a long and ugly conversation. A point counterpoint song and dance that stretches until the following morning. It's grueling and hideous and as the sun creeps over the horizon we find ourselves staring at each other with faces like whitewashed billboards. Numb. Exhausted. But also secure in the knowledge that we don't exist.

Then comes a period of isolation and sadness. There's the occasional outburst of rage when we run mad through the streets at midnight cursing our creator and screaming at the sky. But in general it's a quiet and melancholy time. Veronica quits her job at the club and we live frugally off the money we've squirreled away. I ditch my dump and move into her place.

We never leave the apartment. We order takeout every night. We stare out the window at the falling rain. We cry a lot. We play cards incessantly. We listen to the jazz station and chain-smoke cigarettes. We do puzzles and build model airplanes. We become lethargic and lazy. We dump our brains in the compost pile so we don't have to think.

Days become weeks. Weeks turn into months. Time stretches like a stick of fresh taffy. But through it all we have each other. And there's comfort to be found in our shared dilemma. By the time spring rolls around we've grown very close. We've learned to love each other in ways we never thought possible. We've built something out of the rubble. Our new lives are turning from tolerable to enjoyable.

We take to reading philosophy for kicks. We find it hilarious that real people suffer the same crisis we do. We sit at our favorite coffee shops and argue over the ideas of Kant. We curl up in bed and take turns reading Voltaire. We sit on park benches and discuss Aristotle while the birds sing and the sun warms our faces. We wander the streets at dawn smoking cigarettes and screaming Nietzsche into the pale sky.

What is it we've learned? What conclusions have we arrived at? What truths have we uncovered? That we're lucky. That we're better off. That we've been offered a loophole through which we can avoid some of mankind's nagging dilemmas.

And so we come to cherish our new state. Nonexistence proves to be a kick in the pants. Our decisions are predetermined but along with our freewill goes all feelings of guilt and shame and regret. It's a worthwhile tradeoff. We do exactly as we please because we're no longer accountable for our actions. We shed our inhibitions like a layer of useless skin. We enter into a time of unparalleled hedonism. We roam the city like golden angels.

Our sex life grows by leaps and bounds. Not that it was hurting before. But suddenly everything is acceptable. Nothing is taboo. We feel liberated in the knowledge that nothing we do reflects upon us. No fantasy needs explaining. No fetish needs justifying. No perversion needs discussing.

We start having sex in public places. I bang her in the entryway of our apartment building. We do it in a parking lot behind a Texaco gas station. She gives me head under the tablecloth at out favorite restaurant. I eat her pussy in the back room of a coffee shop. We fuck in restrooms. We fuck in movie theaters. We fuck in alleys. We fuck in the park. We fuck in a hospital waiting room. In a library. In a playground. In a chicken coupe. In a junkyard.

You name it and we try it. I start titty-fucking her. We get into anal sex. We give bondage a whirl. We dabble in asphyxiation. We piss on each other. We beat each other with belts. I clamp clothespins on her nipples. She gives me hummers while fingering my ass. She pours chocolate syrup on my cock. I slather ice cream all over her pussy. I eat Mexican food off her ass. We jimmy-rig contraptions and do it hanging upside down like two bugs on a milkweed plant.

But hedonism's a critter with a thousand different faces and our sex life isn't the only thing effected by it. It gets everywhere. It's messy. It's like cheap sex lube. You squirt a little dab and do the deed. But in the morning the sheets are stained the walls are smudged and your balls are all sticky.

We start drinking like fish. For days on end we keep a steady flow of booze pouring down our throats. We suck up every ounce of liquor we can get our hands on. Anything that gets us drunk. Anything that makes our heads spin like crystal balls and strips the cobwebs from our spines. Anything that takes the harsh edges off the world around us and makes everything soft and fuzzy like a cartoon dream. Anything that gives us the inclination to lie down in the park at night and stare up at the stars. Anything that makes the bums look like angels and the trees look like elephants.

There ceases to be a line between sobriety and intoxication. It becomes just one long ride. A roller coaster screaming up into the heavens then dropping down like a meteor racing to the earth. And just when I think it's over I feel that familiar chug-chug-chug and we start our next ascent into the sky.

Up where the gods are beer-bellied warriors and the women are immaculate hags. Up where the gutter monkeys and sewer trash can wash their sins in buckets of rain and rinse their mouths with the blood of the swine. Then we reach the top and relish in that brief moment of poised silence when everything is perfect and exciting and hilarious. And I piss on all that is below me and giggle as the river of urine chases all the ant-people through their sad little maze of bullshit buildings.

Then comes the thrilling swoosh as I fly down like a bolt of lightening into the streets with Veronica on my arm. Through the night we roam. Both of us wobbling and laughing and staring at the neon lights until we find the bar we're looking for. Then we stroll into the warmth and the noise and the smell.

We grab a booth. We order a pitcher. We chain-smoke cigarettes. We listen to the magical banter of an army of useless drunks. "Great ass." "Why don't I live in a swamp?" "I could totally build a fucking motorcycle." "Why haven't I moved to Alaska already?" And it eventually blends together. Into a song. Into a joke. Into a rant. Into a long and mind-bending poem. And I toss back the rest of the pitcher and throw a nickel in the jukebox then grab Veronica and twirl hysterically across the dance floor while the entire world melts like ice-cream in a broken freezer.

And of course there's drug use. Reefer. Benzedrine. Cheap cocaine. Pills of all shapes and sizes and colors. Uppers. Downers. Screamers. Laughers. We don't care. We just take a walk to the right alley at the right time of night and there's our man standing in the shadows with his bloodshot eyes and his shiny gold chains. He's a black guy named Otis who wears tight collared shirts and checkered slacks and alligator shoes. His skin is darker than the inside of a coal mine and whenever we approach we see nothing but his big toothy grin floating in the air like box of chalk.

"What'll it be tonight" he says as we walk up?

"What do you got" is our usual response?

"Shit man. What don't I got? I got the nose candy that'll make you randy. I got the smoke that'll make you choke. I got the pills that give the thrills. And I got the shit that'll get you lit."

"I think I'll try some of each."

"Step back jack" he says flashing that blinding grin. "Looks like I'm closing early tonight."

I slip him some cash. He slips me the goodies. And that's all there is to it. Some nights we pop the pills right there and take a pull from Otis' flask to wash them down. Then it's off to the races. We hurry home and crank the up jazz just as the shit is hitting our heads. And we curl up on the couch and carry on mad conversations while the ceiling melts and the walls ejaculate and the floor opens up like spread-eagled whore.

And it's on one of these wild nights while I stand wired in front of the bedroom mirror that all the ghosts from my fraudulent past are finally laid to rest. There in the mirror I see the old woman I killed in Korea. But she isn't alone. She's brought everyone with her. Everyone I've wronged or killed or maimed or beaten. They've all come to exonerate me of my sins. To wash the blood from my hands. To siphon the guilt from my heart like a kid stealing gas from a stranger's car. To let me know that they know I had nothing to do with it.

I stumble out of the bedroom and find Veronica mixing some drinks in the kitchen. She's wearing a blissful expression and her hips are swaying to the sound of a Sonny Rollins record. I come up behind her and place my hands on her waist.

"Guess what" I whisper?

"What?"

"Some old acquaintances of mine stopped by and said hi."

"Did you have a nice visit" she asks and I know that she understands?

"I did" I say. "In fact I want to celebrate."

"You name it."

"Not afraid of heights are you?"

"Why" she asks but I'm already out the window and half way up the fire escape?

By the time Veronica reaches the roof I'm naked. The air is cool and the breeze feels like friendly spiders dancing all over my skin. Without a word of prompting she begins to undress. Her body appears white as snow beneath the light of the moon. We can hear the music coming from our apartment and as she steps into my arms the roof top becomes our ballroom.

We dance naked through the moonlight to the sound of Sonny Rollins. We experience for the first time what it means to be free. We have never lived. We will never die. We have no past. We have no future. Nothing matters except for the flesh and the drugs and the booze and the jazz and the moonlight and the idea of a perfect and meaningless eternity.

CHAPTER 11

▼

I'M JUST SHAKING MY TALLY-WHACKER OFF AND WONDERING WHAT ALL THE HUBBUB'S ABOUT

Is there such a thing as too much? I used to believe so. Too much beer and I'd spew chunks. Too much reefer and I'd lose my cool. Too much Mexican food and I'd get the shits. Too much jerking off and my dick would get raw. Too much sinning and I'd worry about hell. Too much flirting and I'd get slapped in the face. Too much speed and the car would start wobbling. Too much sex and I'd catch a dirty disease. Everything I did was regulated by the fear of too much. I was trapped inside my own limitations like a rat in a cage.

Is there such a thing as too much? I used to believe so. Of course I used to believe in Santa Clause as well. And the Easter bunny. And the tooth fairy. And the Green Hornet. And Captain Marvel. And all that other shit that slips away from the party without saying goodbye.

Is there such a thing as too much? I used to believe so. But not anymore. Too much is a scapegoat. Too much is an excuse. Too much is a ghost story to keep children from wandering into the woods alone. Too much is a safety nest for yellowbellies and chicken-shits. Too much is a sugar-tit for pansies and candy-asses.

Too much is the slow lane. Too much is the shallow end. Too much is decaf. Too much is low fat. Too much is condoms. Too much is waiting a half-hour to go swimming after you eat. Too much ain't nothing but a wheelbarrow full of bullshit.

Is there such a thing as too much? No way. Tug off until you're cross-eyed and your palms get hairy. Drive like a hillbilly running moonshine. Hump until your privates need icing. Drink every ounce of booze you can get your hands on. Eat every meal as if it were your last. Approach every fistfight as though it's the bum who raped your mother. Run full speed into the mouth of madness. Run like a mother scratcher until your feet are broken and you're hobbling on your splintered shins.

Is there such a thing as too much? Fuck no. And tonight we hunt down all the naysayers and put them out of their misery. Tonight Veronica and I spit our new religion like a spontaneous poem. Tonight we roam the earth in search of an experience that can only be shared by two people who know they don't exist and who no longer give a shit.

First we hit a Japanese place for dinner. We order bottles of sake. Plates of fish. Dishes of noodles. Bowls of steaming soup. You name it we order it. Every God damned thing on the menu. And when we're done pigging out we just dash out of the joint and run laughing drunk and hysterical around the corner and off into the night.

We stumble into a bar downtown. Some nameless hole in the wall where the drinks are stiff and everybody leaves their worries at the door. We're popping pills and tossing back shots of whiskey. We're dropping coins in the jukebox and singing along. We're laughing and yelling and inviting everyone to march with us on our twisted little scavenger hunt.

We end up in the restroom and I get Veronica bent over the toilet. Her skirt's pulled up around her waist and her panties are pushed to the side. She's got her hands braced against the wall and I'm gripping her hips and hammering away. It's hot. It's sexy. It's pure adrenalin. And we're both coming and screaming and smiling like angels.

Then we're at another bar downtown. Some swanky joint with chandeliers and tablecloths and waiters all gussied up in demeaning little monkey suits. And the drinks cost an arm and a leg but we don't give a rat's ass because we don't plan on paying for them anyway.

And the band's playing some old John Kirby tune that I've always loved. So I grab Veronica and hit the floor. We spin and dip and twirl around. We feel the world crumble around us. We watch as the walls bleed together. We listen to the night serenading the drunken masses. Then I bump into someone and turn to see the face of some disgruntled old fuck giving me the stink eye.

"Watch where you're going" he says. "I'm trying to dance."

I hall off and belt him in the chin. Just for kicks. Just to see the look on his face. Just to hear the sound he makes when he hits the floor. But then the little monkeys are charging at me and I hall off and belt one of them as well. Veronica's laughing and I'm stumbling around throwing punches and then we're holding hands and running out the back door.

Now we're in the middle of the street. And the sky is smiling. And the night is watching. And the cars are swerving. And Veronica's singing. And I'm pulling my cock out and pissing a smiley face in the middle of the road. There's horns honking. There's people yelling. There's brakes squealing. And I'm just shaking my tally-whacker off and wondering what all the hubbub's about.

Then we're back in my Cadillac and we drive to this late night barbeque joint and pick up a bucket of chicken wings to go. We head to the outskirts of town and park on a bridge running over the Mississippi. We sit there listening to the radio and eating chicken and digging the city lights shimmering on the water. Everything is cool. Everything is perfect. Everything is senseless.

"You feel like getting wet" I ask as I finish off the last piece of chicken?

"I always feel like getting wet" she says. "What'd you have in mind?"

"Taking a swim" I say as I fire up a smoke.

"You serious" she asks?

"Of course I am. Are you in?"

"Is a frog's ass water tight" she replies with a smile?

So we step out of the car and start stripping down. The late night air is cool against our skin. The stars are flickering overhead like a million angels with poorly wired porch lights. Crickets and frogs sing their lullaby from the river below. A car races somewhere in the distance. The entire world spins helpless through time and space and we stand here naked going nowhere fast.

"After you" she says.

"Ladies first" I say and flick my cigarette over the bridge. "I insist."

"Hell no. I'm not going first."

"How about together" I ask?

"Together" she agrees.

We take each other's hand and crawl up onto the railing. We take deep breaths and stare out into the night. We step off into nothing and fall through the darkness. We sacrifice ourselves to the empty sky.

Do I believe there's such a thing as too much? I guess I do after all. But not in the same way I used to. It's no longer something to shy away from. It's something to strive for. It's the goal. It's the finish line. It's the pot of gold at the end of the rainbow. It's the grass on the other side of the fence. It's the town just over the hump in the road. Too much is a perfect high. Too much is a never-ending orgasm. Too much is a first round knockout. Too much is true love. Too much is jazz music. Too much is poetry. Too much is the first kiss in the morning. Too much is the last shot of booze before closing. Too much is a young boy's first skin mag. Too much is an old man's last breath. Too much is an idea. Too much is a prayer. Too much is a tasteless joke. Too much is a safe house for all the losers and derelicts who have no place left to go.

CHAPTER 12

▼

STARING CROSS-EYED INTO A PINBALL MACHINE

I wake up at four in the afternoon sick as a dog. The cheap wine has taken its toll. My head feels like a pimple that needs popping and my asshole itches so bad I want to fist myself with a sandpaper glove. I stumble into the bathroom and take a shit. One of those good hung-over dumps when it just falls right out of you. So relaxing in fact that I fall asleep and the next thing I know Veronica's in the kitchen making noise and it's five-thirty and I'm still on the can with my drawers around my ankles.

I step into the shower and holler for Veronica to bring me a beer. When I finish it I ask her to bring me another one. She does. Then another one. By the time the shower is done I've downed an entire six pack and I'm feeling drunk.

I step out of the tub and slip and fall on my back. My head smacks the tile hard. I call for help and Veronica hurries into the bathroom and kneels down beside me. She cradles my head and gently traces her finger over my face.

It feels nice but when she pulls me to my feet I catch a glimpse of myself in the mirror and realize what she's been doing. She's painted my face with my own blood. It's a huge smiley face. I look like a clown. It's awkward for a moment but then we both start to laugh and everything is cool.

We fix up my head then step out to a bar. The place is called The Rubber Monkey. It's nothing fancy. Just a beat little dive where the drinks are cheap and the broads are even cheaper. The bartender is an overweight bum named Tiny who has a chip on his shoulder because his left eye is lazy and his right hand is missing a couple digits. He paces back and forth with a pathetic scowl on his face pouring beer and whiskey for all the hollow-eyed zombies who sit hunched over their bowls of free peanuts.

I order a couple of shots and a pitcher of beer than sit down with Veronica at a booth toward the back. A little later I'm milking a pretty good buzz and decide to smoke a joint. I fire the thing up but about half way through Tiny starts eye-balling me from the bar.

"Hey" he shouts. "You better not be smoking what I thing you're smoking."

"Don't sweat" I reply. "It's only marijuana."

"Well put it out you smart ass son of a bitch."

"Why don't you come make me" I yell.

"I'll teach you to get smart with me" he says and comes out from around the bar holding a baseball bat.

"What the hell are you doing" Veronica asks as we watch him approach?

"I thought another bar brawl sounded like fun" I say. "That's all."

And when he gets close to me I stand up and face him. He takes a swing with his bat but I duck it and throw a heavy punch that catches him right in the kisser. He falls to his knees and I bust a chair over his back. Then I'm getting bum rushed by a few of the regulars. I grab a pitcher of beer and toss it in the first guy's face. He rubs his eyes and I punch him in the gut. But then the others are on top of me. Next thing I know I'm sliding down the bar on my belly busting glasses with my head. It hurts like hell but I can't for the life of me wipe the shit-eating grin off my face. I manage to get to my feet and find Veronica and as we run out the door the sound of our laughter flutters up into the night like a gaggle of ridiculous birds.

We pile in my Caddy and cruise the strip until we decide we need some more drugs. I hang a right and lay rubber in the direction of Oris. As always we find him chilling on the corner with his slick duds and his shinny white smile glowing like a neon sign. He fires up a joint and we all smoke it and talk shop. He says he's holding some good cocaine so we buy a bag and pass it around taking gummers.

Then we take off and my face is so numb I have to keep checking the rearview mirror to make sure I'm not drooling on myself. We hit a liquor store and pick up some whiskey then roll through town taking swigs from the bottle and doing lines off the dashboard. The Caddy seems to drive itself and so I just crank on the radio and lean back in my seat and let my hand slide up Veronica's thigh. She leans over and kisses me and the taste of her mouth is a perfect blend of whiskey and drugs and cheap lipstick. I roll down the window to smoke a cigarette and the breeze rushing in feels like invisible angels running their fingers through my hair and tickling my skin with their tongues.

By the time we hit downtown we're so smashed on booze and coke that we don't know our asses from two holes in the ground. Driving my Caddy through the busy streets is like staring cross-eyed into a pinball machine. And before I know it I run a red light.

I swerve to miss the oncoming traffic but then jump a curb and slam into a mail box. Someone on the sidewalk starts cussing at me so I give him the bird and throw the empty bottle of whiskey at his face. Then I hear a siren and see flashing lights coming up the street. I jam it into first and take off up the sidewalk. Pedestrians jump out of the way like little squirrels trying to cross the highway. A fat man eating a hotdog dives behind a dumpster. A middle-aged barfly yanks her friend out of the way and looks like two kids plying crack the whip. Some drunk hobo crawls up a tree. An old man swings his cane at my windshield.

When I see an alley on my right I turn and cross under a railroad bridge then smash through a fence and cut across a parking lot. By the time we hit the highway the copper's long gone so I drop it into high gear and charge off into the night.

A little later as we're racing down some dark highway outside of town a killer Ben Webster tune called "Cadillac Slim" comes on the radio. It's one of Veronica's favorite old jazz songs and she gets the wild idea to ride on top of the car while it plays. I pull over and after she crawls up on the hood I turn the music up full blast then gun it down the highway.

We're doing about thirty-five when I hit a pothole. The car jumps and skids. Veronica's knees buckle and she falls on the hood then goes sailing off onto the side of the road.

I skid to a stop and run over to see if she's all right. She's lying all tangled up at the bottom of a muddy ditch. But to my surprise she's fine. In fact she's laughing hysterically. I start laughing too and before I know it I'm down next to her in the ditch. We start kissing and groping and smearing mud all over each other's bodies.

Then we're naked and she's fingering herself and jerking me off with the slippery mud. I lean back and close my eyes. In my mind I see only Veronica kneeling in the mud fingering herself and jerking me off.

This is when I realize there's no longer any difference between our thoughts and the world around us. We've surrendered so thoroughly to our fantasies that the two have become interwoven. We have no more secrets. We have no privacy. We have no place left to hide. We've thrown our singularity onto the ground like chicken feed and let everyone swarm and peck and devour it. But just as this thought occurs to me I climax and all is forgotten in the chaos and bliss of another exquisitely filthy orgasm.

CHAPTER 13

▼

OUR TEETH BEGINNING TO ROT AND FALL OUT

Discovering that I didn't exist was a lot like being born. Of course there was no mother with her legs in the air trying to squeeze me out. There was no father to welcome me into the world with a soothing voice. There was no doctor to catch me and wipe the slop from my face. But all said and done the outcome was about the same. I had become like a child.

And children don't know when to stop. They haven't developed the instinct that tells them how far is too far. Give them some cotton candy and they'll eat until they're sick as a dog and pissing pink sugar out their ass. They learn to beat off and they do it five or six times a day. They get a stuffed animal for Christmas and they drag it everywhere until the damned thing's just a lumpy sack of dirty fur.

This is what's happened to Veronica and I. We've become kids in a world of parentless excess. We have no one to put us to bed. No one to take our candy away. No one to make us eat our greens. No one to tan our hides when we do something stupid. Our world is just a huge sugar-tit and we keep sucking it despite our teeth beginning to rot and fall out.

But the seasons come and go. The pendulum always swings. The leaves fall. The rivers freeze. The teenagers fuck. The old people die. And it isn't long before things turn around.

It happens at a greasy jazz joint downtown. The place is packed and the band on stage is wailing something furious. Everyone is jumping. As always Veronica and I are on the dance floor strung-out and sloshed on liquor. But tonight it's too much. Too many sweaty bodies pressing in from all directions. Too much smoke hanging in the air. Too many screaming voices. Too many slamming drums. Too many piercing horns.

I feel sick and weak and know I'm coming down. But I'm not ready to call it a night. So I park Veronica at the bar with a pitcher of beer and work the joint looking to score. I see a shady looking Mexican guy shooting stick in the back of the bar. He's pushing six-four and built like a work mule. His attire is part hobo part Hollywood fruit. A bright orange sport shirt and a pair of corduroy slacks that might have fit him when he was fourteen. He has a crooked nose and a couple of metal teeth. He doesn't look pleased that I'm approaching him.

"Holding anything" I ask?

"Take a walk man" he says. "I ain't talking to no fucking cop."

"Who do I look like? Joe Friday?"

"I suppose you're right" he says sizing me up. "You're too fucked up looking to be a cop."

"Thanks" I say mockingly. "Now what do you got?"

He pulls a baggie of cocaine out of his boot. It's dirty and yellow. But cheap as hell. I don't complain. I slip him some coin then pocket the bag and make my way to the restroom.

Once inside I lock myself in the far stall and start dumping some coke on the toilet lid. My hands are shaking so bad I can hardly cut it into lines or roll a dollar bill. I drop to my knees and start snorting like a pig. It burns my nose but I keep going hoping to catch a high. Line after line after line. Then it hits me all at once. My face freezes. Vomit flies out of my mouth. My heart does cartwheels in my chest. My nose starts to bleed.

And this is when it happens. This is when everything changes. Only at this moment of complete abandonment am I able to see things as they actually are. I look down at my body all covered with puke and blood and I know that I can sink no further. I know that I've hit rock bottom. I'm out of options. I'm desperate. But with desperation comes a sense of clarity. Urgency breeds ingenuity.

And this is when I see the graffiti on the stall wall. It reads "is man only a blunder of God or God only a blunder of man?"

My mind is starving and frantic and this quote is just enough to trigger something inside. I'm flooded with a surge of memories. For the first time in a great while I think of Gerald Oscar Davidson. I recall all the events leading up to the moment I met him. I remember the conversation we had on that night. We discussed the mystery novel he's writing. The mystery novel that I'm starring in.

Everything comes together at this moment. Everything crystallizes. Everything congeals. Everything explodes in a big orgy of synchronicity. I have an idea. A plan. A way out.

If I'm the main character in a mystery novel then why have I been spending so much time doing nothing but fucking and drinking? Why am I laying on the floor of a men's room covered in my own throw-up?

I realize that I can determine the outcome of the book. I have control of my actions. And if I have control of my actions it means I have some control of Gerald Oscar Davidson as well. I can influence his mind. I can take it over completely. I can escape from the book. I can become real?

I grab a hold of the toilet and pull myself onto my feet. My vision is blurry. My legs are wobbly. My head is throbbing. But inside I feel better than I have in a long time. I leave the stall then kick open the restroom door and walk out into the crowded nightclub.

Everyone stares. Everyone points. I'm the freak. I'm the monster. I'm the honkey with the vomit stains and the bloody nose. Not that I care. I walk through the bar with my head held high. I'm proud of my blood and my puke. They're medals of honor. They're souvenirs from my descent into pure debauchery. They're collectables from the edge of nowhere. They're tickets out of this world of make-believe.

Veronica's sitting at the bar where I left her. I put my arm around her and together we walk outside. The fresh night air is sobering. I suck it in greedily. I pull Veronica to me and hold her tight. She feels insubstantial in my arms. Almost like she isn't there at all. Almost like I'm hugging myself.

I stare up into the starry sky and feel shame for what we've done. It's an emotion I haven't felt for so long that it takes a moment to understand what it is. I kiss Veronica on the forehead then open the car door and put her in. I crawl in next to her and fire it up.

When we get home I dim the lights and run a hot bath. We hunker down in the water and the steam and the candle light. We hold each other. We relax. We melt. We dissolve.

And as the faucet drips and the seconds tick by our bath grows in significance. It becomes symbolic. It takes on a dual meaning. We're not only washing our bodies we're cleaning our insides as well. We scrub away the grime that's collected in our hearts. We purge ourselves of all the booze and drugs and nihilistic rhetoric. We sweat out all the filth and junk and hedonistic tendencies that have gathered up inside us.

"What happened back there at the club" Veronica asks with her eyes closed and her mouth just above the water?

"Nothing we hadn't known was coming" I answer.

"Whatever happened I'm glad it happened" she says. "I was getting tired. Real tired."

"I know what you mean" I whisper.

"Buckley?"

"Yea?

"I'm scared" she says.

"Don't be."

"But what are we going to do" she asks?

"I have a plan" but that's all I say because I don't know if it's going to work and I don't know how she fits into it.

"I love you" she says with her eyes still closed.

"I love you too."

When the bath is done I carry Veronica into bed. I crawl in beside her. She falls asleep instantly. I do not. I'm too exhausted to sleep. I'm beyond it. My mind is a jail cell and my thoughts are inmates packed in tight and pacing nervously.

Then the crying comes. I bite my fist to kill the sound. It's a clean cry though. A comforting cry. I'm exhausted and sad. But I know who I am. I know where I stand. I know what the score is. I scoot up against Veronica's warm naked body and fall asleep with tears still pouring out my eyes.

We sleep late into the following day. And when we finally wake up the first thing we do is make sweet love for a long time. Afterwards Veronica runs to the store for bagels and coffee and we have breakfast in bed and listen to the radio. We make love again then fall back asleep to an old Buck Clayton tune.

When I wake up it's early evening and I can't remember feeling so well rested. Veronica is sound asleep and the radio is still quietly playing. I look out the window and see the sun sinking over the rooftops in the distance. It's beautiful. It fills me with hope. It tells me that the time has come.

I get out of bed and stroll into the bathroom. I shave and brush my teeth then get dressed. I take my time. I cherish the stillness and the intensity of the moment. My movements are precise and purposeful. Once I'm dressed I comb my hair then walk to side of the bed where Veronica is sleeping. I look down at her face and in the dim red light of the setting sun it seems to melt into the shadowy sheets. I kneel down and kiss her lips.

"Hey" she says as she opens her eyes.

"Hey" is my response.

"You look sharp. What's the occasion?"

"I have to go see somebody."

"What for" she asks?

"Me and him got a few things we need straightening out."

Then I stand up and walk out of the room. The first step on my way back to the house of Gerald Oscar Davidson. Back to my master. Back to my slave. To my creator. To my enemy. My origin. My conclusion. Fate. Mortality. God.

PART III

CHAPTER 14

▼

JUST A TWO BIT DRUNKEN CRIME WRITER IN A TRUST FUND SUIT

It's dark by the time I reach the home of Gerald Oscar Davidson. All the houses along Maple Lane are lit up like jack-o-lanterns on Halloween night. I step out of my car and notice a heavy silence hanging over the street. It weighs me down like a burdensome lover with too much baggage. The whole scene is surreal. It feels as if I'm in the middle of two worlds. As if by wanting to bridge the gap between fiction and reality I'm wandering into some dark void that isn't one or the other.

I reach the top of the driveway then walk up the front steps and knock. Gerald opens the door a few moments later. His hair is greasy and thick with dandruff. His skin seems to droop from his bones. His eyes look like two rotting knotholes in a dead oak tree. His posture is that of an overcooked noodle. Yet despite his haggard demeanor he's sporting some sharp threads. The combination only makes him appear desperate and fraudulent. Just a two bit drunken crime writer in a trust fund suit.

My presence seems to unnerve him. He blinks as if in disbelief. He runs his fingers through his greasy hair. He fiddles with his mustache. He shifts from side to side. He clears his throat. He adjusts his collar. He sticks his hands in his pockets.

"You gonna invite me in" I ask staring him right in the bloodshot eyes? "Or we gonna do this out here in the driveway for the neighbors to watch?"

"Of course" he says stepping aside and motioning me in. "I've been expecting you."

"Sure you have."

"How could I not have" he says with a short burst of condescending laughter? "I've already written this chapter."

"Then tell me why I'm here."

"That's easy" he says. "You're here to take over my mind."

"You're damned right" I say.

"Of course I'm right. I wrote it."

"I know you wrote it" I say. "But it was my idea."

"No it wasn't" he says but something in his voice tells me I'm hitting a nerve.

"Yes it was" I continue. "You were fine with me just rotting away. You were fine with me drinking myself into oblivion. But I wasn't. So I thought of a way to get out."

"This is not your idea" he says. "I came up with this. This is my story. This is my plot."

"Your plot was weak" I say. "You set out to write a mystery novel but your clues were so easy that I solved the damned thing within a few chapters."

"You still don't get it do you? You haven't solved anything. And you never will either. You don't exist. You're just ink on paper. You're just an idea of mine. You're just a part of me. A facet of my brain."

"That's it" I exclaim. "You said it."

"Said what" he asks?

"That I'm a part of you. That I'm a facet of your brain."

"So what" he says? "You are. That's all you are."

"That's all I need to be" I respond.

We walk down the hallway and into the den. A stained glass floor lamp sits in the corner. Its glow is subdued. It gives off just enough light to survey the room. The joint is even messier than before. More wine bottles. More cigarette butts. More dirty dishes. More everything. It goes beyond mere disorder. The place feels crazy. As if Gerald has spent so much time here that the room itself has become saturated with his lunacy. I can almost see it coming up off the floor like heat shimmering on the highway.

Gerald drops onto the couch. He lets out an exhausted sigh. It looks as if the interaction is already taking a toll. Already wearing him thin. I brush some trash onto the floor and take a seat in the chair facing the couch. I scoot up close and get right in his face.

"You've already admitted that I'm a part of you" I continue. "That's half the battle right there."

"How's that" he asks?

"Because you're admitting that you're insane."

"No I'm not."

"Yes you are" I say. "You've admitted that I'm part of you. And yet you've written another chapter in which we keep having conversations. That means you're talking to yourself. You're fucking crazy."

"Please stop" he says closing his eyes.

I delight in his plea. I lean back in my chair and watch him with a satisfied smile. It seems as though it's going to be easier than I had thought. But to my disappointment he regains his composure and struggles onward.

"I am an artist and an intellectual" he says. "And you're right. I did set out to write a mystery novel. However you're wrong about the plot being weak. I intentionally had you solve the mystery early because I was more interested in how you would respond to the burdensome knowledge that you do not exist. I don't want this book to fit into any particular box. I want this book to start off as one thing and end up something else. A book that reads like crime noir but is actually a statement on existence and the way we perceive reality. And that's what you fail to understand. That this is all well thought out. That this is a controlled and disciplined work of art. You have no control whatsoever over the outcome of this novel. You've just been written to believe that you do."

I let it wash over me. I let it sink in. He talks a fancy game. But his words don't amount to much. I know in my heart that I'm right. And I know he knows it too. We sit here staring at each other. The tension hangs in the air between us like a stink you don't want to breathe. I use the time to look Gerald over. He looks confused and tired. I can tell the conversation is draining him. He leans down low in the couch and closes his eyes.

"You're bluffing" I say hoping to wear him down even more.

"That's you're opinion."

"You're right" I say. "That is my opinion. It's also my opinion that you learned a lot of fancy words and highbrow rhetoric from your art school friends in New York. But that doesn't change the fact that you live like a pig and get in arguments with yourself."

"As for the state of my living quarters" he says struggling to sit upright. "It's true. I have indeed neglected my domestic duties. But what's the fun of being a writer if you can't play the role of the slovenly recluse. Besides. When you have as much money as I do you're no longer a slob. You're just eclectic. And as for the conversations I carry on with myself. It's just part of my creative process. Just one of the techniques I employ to facilitate a healthy flow of ideas."

Again a silence rises up between us. It's thick and palpable. A wall of petrified tension. I lean back in my chair and analyze his words. He's trying hard to appear calm. Too hard. It comes off desperate and contrived. In the end it only furthers my belief that he's holding on to his sanity by the thinnest of threads. I lean forward in my chair and press on unmercifully.

"I think you're jealous" I state frankly. "I think I'm everything you want to be. I think you created me as an answer to your own shortcomings. I think you need an alter ego to help you forget your own insecurities."

"That's preposterous" he mutters.

"Oh really? Then why am I dating the girl from New York who you were too shy to even talk to?"

And as I speak I notice just how flimsy the barrier is that separates our two identities. It feels as if his consciousness has become permeable. As if I'm suddenly able to reach inside his mind and steal his secrets. To pull them out and use them to my own advantage. I understand that I'm no longer speculating. No longer guessing. I'm speaking the truth.

"Why is it I look just like your younger brother" I ask? "The younger brother that you envied growing up. The younger brother that you wanted so badly to resemble."

Gerald is starting to shake slightly. A subtle tremble. Like a child who has played too long in the snow. Also his face is flushed and red. I can tell he isn't too fond of me rooting around inside his noggin for private dirt to throw in his face. But he's so out of it that he's incapable of stopping me. An abusive master in disbelief that his dog had finally bit back.

"And you always hated growing up in Louisiana. You always wanted to be someplace glamorous and exciting. And that's why I was born in L.A.. Admit it. My life is everything that you wish yours was."

But Gerald is too out of it. He's gone. The conversation has worn him out completely. He looks as if he has aged ten years in the last fifteen minutes. He's sunk down in the couch with his chin on his chest. Like a washed-up prize fighter slumped on a stool in the corner of the ring waiting for the bell so he can collect his next beating.

With Gerald nodded out there's nothing more I can do. I decide to call it a night. I pull myself out of the chair and stand up.

"Don't worry" I say to his sprawled and pathetic shape. "I'll be back soon."

I take my time driving home. Cruise around awhile smoking cigarettes and digging the late night streets. The night owls. The empty windows. The neon signs. The alley cats. The steam rising out of the manholes like transient ghosts trying to hitch a ride somewhere. I see a shooting star blaze a crooked trail across the big black sky. I see a homeless fellow getting rolled for change by a couple of drunks. I see a hooker getting into the back seat of a long white Pontiac. I see a kid in a hotrod showing off for a couple of tinny bopper chicks by laying rubber at a stop light. And I just roll through it all listening to the radio and trying to recollect a time when I didn't have to wonder what was real and what wasn't.

When I get to the pad I let myself in and tiptoe into the bedroom. The lights are off but the streetlamps are shinning in and I can make out the shape of Veronica's naked body curled up in the sheets like a pale snake. I walk to the bed and pull the sheets away. We don't say a word. We don't need to. Our mouths meet in the darkness and I let my hands run across her flesh. Her nipples get hard and her legs get goose bumps. She pulls me down onto the bed. She takes my clothes off. I enter her. Her pussy is warm and tight. It grips at my cock like the hands of an experienced masseuse. She rolls me onto my back and climbs on top. The streetlights shine in and her hair seems to glow like a golden fire. I put her nipples in my mouth and suck them and bite them and feel them stiffen against my lips. I reach down and grab Veronica's ass with both my hands. I pull myself in deep. She starts to climax and I pull out and roll her over onto her back. I spread her legs and put my mouth down against her pussy. She squirms and gasps and grabs the back of my head. I squeeze her ass cheeks and taste her cum. Then it's my turn. She goes down on me nice and slow. I feel the orgasm coming a mile away. I place my hands on the side of her face and feel her mouth open and close as my load shoots down her throat. We collapse together under the sheets in a pile of sweat and sperm.

"Buckley" she says a few minutes later as we lay in the darkness with her head on my chest. "Do you think we can ever be happy knowing that we don't exist?"

"I'm always happy when I'm with you Veronica."

"I know" she says. "But I mean do you think we can ever learn to forget about it and just lead normal lives?"

"No" I say frankly.

"Buckley" she says after a couple minutes. "If you had to put money on it would you say there's a God?"

"I suppose" I say.

"And do you think that God has already decided the fate of everything?"

"I don't know" I say. "Why do you ask?"

"Because I was thinking that if there's a God and he's already decided everything then there's really no difference between us and everyone else."

"Except we know for a fact that we don't exist" I say. "Everyone else still believes that their lives really matter. That their actions mean something. They still have the illusion of freedom."

"But what is freedom" she asks? "What does it really mean to be free?"

"What's all this about" I ask? "Where are all these questions coming from?"

She doesn't answer.

"Does this have to do with where I was earlier tonight" I ask? "Does this have to do with Gerald Oscar Davidson?"

"Buckley" she says. "I don't exactly know what you're up to. And I don't care either. I know you have to do what you have to do. It's just that."

"It's just that what" I ask?

"It's just that I don't want to loose you" she says. "I'm not going to loose you am I?"

"Listen Veronica" I say holding her naked body tight against mine. "I don't exactly know what I'm doing either. But I do know we're going to make it through this. Somehow we're going to be together forever. I promise."

About an hour later I'm still wide awake so I slip out of bed nice and easy and go into the living room. I thumb through her stack of records until I find a classic Bunk Johnson album then toss it on. The music is like a mouthful of valium. I feel the tension drain from my body the instant it hits my ears. I drop into the chair by the window then fish a smoke out of my pack of Lucky Strikes and spark it up.

I stare out the window. Out into the darkness of the great almighty nowhere. Where an old man with a broken soul sleeps under a leaky roof and pushes a wheelbarrow full of tortured dreams through the nothingness of night. Where tomorrow's poet sits on a fire escape with his journal and a jug of cheap wine smoking hand rolled cigarettes and recording the sounds of the sleeping city. Where a kid races his crotch-rocket through a cornfield under the cold starry sky. Where a rundown old-timer sits hunched over a cup of black coffee at an all-night truck stop and scribbles a love letter to a dame who won't ever read it.

And somewhere out there in this tangled scrap pile called Shreveport is Gerald Oscar Davidson. Huddled like a baby in the safety of night. Not knowing that his enemy is awake and watching. Starving. Drooling. Waiting for the sun to come creeping up over the rooftops. Waiting for the horns to blow and the planets to collide. Waiting for the smell of combat. The taste of blood. The thrill of conquest.

I put my cigarette out in the ashtray and head for bed. Urged by the keen suspicion that the sooner I fall asleep the sooner the next chapter begins.

CHAPTER 15

▼

WHERE THE DAMES ARE EASY AND THE MEN CARRY BLADES IN THEIR BOOTS

I'm back at Gerald's place the very next night. Same scene as before. The sun's down. The neighborhood's quiet. The sidewalks are covered with fallen leaves. A pale moon the shape of a toenail clipping creeps across the autumn sky. A dog barks. A garage door closes. And all the homes are glowing like a string of million dollar Christmas lights.

But things start differently this time around. Gerald doesn't answer the door. I know he's home because his Buick is parked in the driveway so I keep knocking. I knock till my knuckles feel like I'm fist fighting a heavy weight with a cement chin.

I give up and start snooping around the place. Peeking in windows. I find him in the den sitting on the couch. The lighting is piss poor but I can see that his eyes are open. He's not asleep. He's just ignoring me. I pound on the window and holler his name.

"Go away" he finally yells. "I'm not playing this game anymore."

"This isn't a game" I yell back.

"Go away" he screams placing his hands over his ears. "I'm not listening to you."

But I know he can still hear me so I keep yelling. I keep banging on the window. I keep messing with his head. And in the end it pays off. He gives up and lets me in.

He opens the door and we just stand there staring. Sizing each other up. He's been drinking again. I can smell it. I can see it in his eyes. I can tell by the way he's moving his mouth like a baby who wants more tit.

We adjourn to the den and begin round two. At first we don't say anything. At least not with our mouths. But our minds are colliding like a couple of horny old Billy goats head-butting for the only piece of tail in the barnyard.

I can feel our brains wrestling. Meshing. Twisting. Dissolving. Dancing. Searching for leverage. Peering into the dark places. Peeling off the scabs. Ripping open the private secrets. And as our psyches struggle in some strange and silent boxing match I feel the two of us overlap into one.

It feels like I'm at the bottom of a dog pile in a vicious brawl. I don't know whose leg I'm biting. I don't know whose face I'm scratching. I don't know whose nuts I'm kicking. All I know is that I'm alive and every part of me wants to stay that way. And so I keep fighting and wailing and holding on to that primal urge that always chooses life over death no matter what the cost.

When I open my eyes I'm covered with sweat and my head's pounding like a cheap tequila hangover. I check my watch and notice an hour has passed. Gerald's still on the couch. He looks rattled and confused. But he's awake. And he's watching me.

"What did you think" he asks with a shaky voice? "That I was just going to roll over and play dead?"

"I did actually" I say.

"Well I hate to break it to you Buckley. But I rather enjoy my life. And I have no intention of relinquishing it to you."

"What about me" I ask? "You think I plan on giving up?"

"That's what I'm hoping."

"Well" I say. "Try shitting in one hand and hoping in the other. See which one fills up first."

"When you say stuff like that you make it real hard to dislike you" he says. "And yet I do."

"But you wrote this" I say. "So you disliking me only proves my point. That you dislike yourself."

"Quit trying to analyze me" he says. "We're beyond that."

"Oh really" I ask? "Then why are we having this conversation? You wrote this didn't you?"

"We both know I wrote this" he replies. "But that's not the point. The point is that this book is not reality."

"What you don't get" I say. "Is that sometimes reality's not black and white. In fact sometimes it's pretty God damned gray."

"Buckley" he says forcing a half-assed grin. "Philosophizing is not your strong-point. But don't worry. It's not your fault. I wrote you that way. Heavy on brawns. Light on brains."

"Who are you to talk about brains" I ask? "You're the one loosing your fucking marbles."

"I'm not losing my mind" he says. "My character is losing his mind. This is all just a book."

"I know this is a book" I reply. "I spent the first nine chapters figuring that out. But I also know that this book is directly tied to you in real life. Why else would you have written yourself into it?"

But he doesn't respond. He just rubs his face and shakes his head. Then he stands up and walks down the hall into the kitchen. He returns holding a bottle of gin. He pours a tall one then drains it straight down his throat. His eyes do cartwheels and his kisser puckers up real ugly like. He pours another one even taller than the first. He downs it in one gulp.

As he works on the bottle of liquor I notice a change come over him. He's got a nervous energy about him now. Like a virgin about to get laid. A crook about to hold up a mart. A rope that's about to snap. Inside his eyes I can see a freaked out intensity. The wired and tightened look of a desperate fiend.

He tosses back the last slug of gin and something about the way he slams the empty glass down on the table tells me things are about to get ugly. Something in his twitchy booze-soaked eyes tells me the gloves are coming off.

Then we get to talking again. I can tell right away my instincts were right. No longer is it some intellectual game of cat and mouse. No longer are we aiming verbal arrows at holes in the other one's psychological armor. No longer are we engaged in a dull debate like two dried-up politicians fussing over tax plans. It's now regressed to a straight up argument. Nothing cute. Nothing clever. Just the two of us having it out like a couple of drunken sailors. Cussing. Screaming. Pacing the room. Circling each other like starving tigers locked in a cage together.

Maybe Gerald is a nasty drunk and those last few gulps of liquor triggered the asshole inside of him. Maybe I'm fed up with looking at his pasty white face and hearing his condescending voice. Or maybe were both just tired of this stupid song and dance and feel that it's time to shit or get off the pot. Truth is I don't know why it gets so heated all of a sudden. Truth is I don't care either. If he wants to dance we'll dance. But we're dancing the way I know how. Not slow and classy like at some highbrow country club. But fast and hard like at a back alley shindig where the dames are easy and the men carry blades in their boots.

"You're too fucking stupid to take over my mind" he says. "You know that right?"

"You think I'm stupid" I growl as I walk towards him? "You couldn't pour piss out of a boot if the instructions were written on the heel."

"Oh you are so fucking clever" he says. "Always rattling off your little sayings."

"They're not mine" I say. "They're yours. You wrote all of this remember? Or were you too wasted at the time? You useless fucking drunk."

"I'm smarter drunk than you are sober" he says. "You're nothing but a pea brained brute."

"Brains have got nothing to do with this" I scream pointblank in his face. "This is about heart. This is about courage. This is about having calluses on your God damned hands. All the stuff you don't know shit about. You sheltered little silver spoon sissy."

"You don't fucking know me" he says.

"Bullshit" I yell. "I'm a part of you. I know everything there is to know."

"Well guess what" he says? "I know you too. I know you from the inside out. I fucking created you."

On and on it goes. This juvenile banter lasts for quite some time. Insults. Putdowns. Threats. They fly around the room like hideous birds with deformed wings. And with each comeback the tension between us builds. Our hatred is a furnace and our words are loads of coal. Hotter and hotter until the pipes start trembling and the bolts rattle loose and the whole thing explodes in a blinding white flash.

"You sure are a cocky piece of shit for someone who doesn't actually exist."

"I do exist" I say jamming my finger into his chest. "I may not be flesh and blood. But I got more life in me than you ever will."

"All you have is what I've given you" he says.

"That's not true."

"It is true" he says. "Without me you'd have nothing. I gave you life. I gave you your name. I even gave you Veronica Vaughn."

"That's fucking bullshit" I yell. "I got Veronica myself. We met and fell in love. You had nothing to do with it."

"Don't kid yourself Buckley" he says. "I've been there the whole time. I know how she likes it. I know what she says when you're slamming her head against the wall in the middle of the night. I know the trick she does with her tongue while she's sucking your cock."

"Why you God damned peeping tom" I scream. "You're nothing but a fucking parasite. A leech. A tic. Getting your kicks by living vicariously through me."

"Fuck you" he yells.

"Fuck you" I yell back.

And that's the final load of coal that causes the furnace to blow. The tension becomes too much and it all just snaps. I leap on Gerald and drag him down. In a couple seconds I'm on top of him pinning him to the ground. I slip my hands around his neck and start choking him.

"I want out of this book" I scream as I wring his neck like a dirty rag. "I want to be real."

But as I squeeze his neck I feel my hands penetrate his skin. It's as if Gerald is a pond and I'm reaching into the water to grab a coin that's resting beneath the surface. Then my arms submerge. Then my chest. My face. My entire body sinks into him. The two of us mesh into one. Everything goes black. And there in the darkness of inner space our minds collide once again.

All forms collapse. All shapes dissolve. All that exists is Gerald and myself entangled in a knot of hatred and rage. It feels like a game of mercy except it's not our hands that are locked together. It's our minds. Our psyches. Our wills. Our souls. Our entire beings. The very essence of who we are as individuals is summoned from the depths and unleashed upon each other like two pit bulls in a ring of money waving spectators.

I can feel the momentum ebb and flow as we struggle for an advantage over the other. Every time I make a push to overcome him my guard drops and I can feel the invisible tendrils of his personality taking me over from the inside out.

I reach the point of complete exhaustion. But just before I give up I feel Gerald start to fade. I seize the moment. I push with all my remaining strength. And for the first time I gain a sense of control. I feel the fire that is his identity fade to a dime flicker. And as he shrinks I notice myself start to grow. Materialize. Become real. I flex my mind and try to wipe him out entirely. But Gerald refuses to let go. He hangs on by just a thread. But that thread is all he needs.

The longer we battle the more obsessed I become. All else is meaningless. Even time itself no longer matters. Hours melt. Minutes dissolve. Seconds flutter away like butterflies chased by children through a summer field. Eventually the fatigue becomes so severe that my consciousness starts to fade. Everything becomes numb. Everything shuts down. I fall spinning into the chaos of my own desperation.

When I open my eyes the room is silent and still. It takes me a long time to figure out where the hell I am. I sit up and check the scene and it all comes back to me in a dizzying blur. Gerald's lying next to me sawing logs. He looks a bit roughed up. I check my watch again. It's a quarter to three in the morning. Shocked at how long I've been out I stand up on wobbly legs. I take a step toward the door. I stop and look down at Gerald Oscar Davidson.

"I'll see you tomorrow" I say and spit right in his sleeping face.

Once again I'm wound too tight to head straight home. I find a little diner and hunker down in a booth with a cup of coffee and a slice of apple pie. The waitress is a short brunette gal with thick ankles and a light mustache. When she's not hustling slop to the tables she's sitting at the counter drinking soda and working on a crossword puzzle. There's a pimply faced teenager sitting in the corner shoveling a banana split down his throat and trying not to cry. I reckon he just got dumped or struck out on a date or caught a beating from his old man. All of which will wet your eyes when you're sixteen and don't know straight up from sickum. There's an old geezer sitting in front of me with a nose like a sausage link and two hands so crippled with arthritis they look like they belong on a claw foot tub. He can't grip his fork worth two-hoots and every time he goes for a bite the food falls on the plate. Finally he just leans forward and eats it like a horse with a feedbag. And as I sit here warming up and watching the faces of all these beat and lonely souls I start sorting a few things out.

I think about Gerald Oscar Davidson. About my plan. About my progress. About my future. He's a stubborn old cocksucker. More than I would have guessed. But it's still looking like my plan just might work out. Things are moving along pretty well. It shouldn't be more than a few more nights before I take over his mind completely.

But that makes time a sparse commodity. I still haven't concocted a scheme which will allow Veronica to come with me. My pants are around my ankles and my tit's caught in the wringer. On one side I got a dame that I have no intention of letting go of. And on the other side I got an overwhelming desire to be real and experience life. I got romance in one hand and a war that needs winning in the other.

When I fail to come up with a solution I become frustrated and give up. I light a cigarette and lean back in the booth. And as I smoke I feel my mood start to change. Suddenly my predicament doesn't seem quite so tight. Suddenly I got a hunch that everything's going to work itself out.

I drop some change on the table then stroll outside and jump in the Caddy. I light another cigarette and take off down the road.

When I get home I'm surprised to find the lights still on in the kitchen. I drop my keys on the coffee table and hang my jacket in the front closet.

"Hey sweetie" I say softly as I walk through the living room. "I'm home."

I round the corner into the kitchen and there's Veronica. She's lying on the floor in a small pool of blood. She's out cold. Her forehead's smashed to hell. It's a got a lump on it the size of a golf ball. I drop to my knees and scoop her up like a child. She stirs slightly and struggles to wake. With her in my arms I rush into the bathroom and start filling up the tub. I undress her and lay her in the bath then grab a washcloth and gently start cleaning her wound.

After I clean it good I run back to the kitchen and put some ice cubes in the washcloth. I hold it to her forehead and slowly the swelling starts to recede. I stroke her hair and kiss her cheek. She opens her eyes and tries to smile.

"You're going to be all right" I say in a soothing voice. "And whoever did this is going to pay."

"That's just the thing" she says as the tears fill her eyes and her voice trails off.

"What is it" I ask? "What happened?"

"I did this to myself" she whispers through her tears.

"What do you mean?"

"I don't know how to explain it" she continues. "Last thing I remember I was in the kitchen making dinner. Then I just started slamming my head against the wall. I couldn't stop. I did it over and over and over. I just kept slamming it against the wall until I passed out."

She begins to sob hysterically. My heart leaps out to her. She looks so vulnerable lying there sad and naked under the stark bathroom light. I lean into the tub and hug her with all my strength. I want to pull her into myself. To hold her there where she'll be loved and safe forever.

"Why did I do it" she asks touching the wound on her head?

"You didn't."

"Yes I did."

"No you didn't" I repeat. "But I got a good idea who did."

CHAPTER 16

▼

A DISGUSTING MOCKERY
OF ALL THINGS HUMAN

Round three starts off with a bang. I'm at his place the next morning. Bright and early. He's got the doors locked and the curtains drawn.

I don't mess around this time. No peeking in windows. No calling his name. No come out come out wherever you are bullshit. I kick the front door wide open. Wood splinters. The lock busts. I barge in the joint like an angry wind.

I find Gerald upstairs in his bedroom. He's sitting on the edge of the bed tying a bathrobe around his waist. His face is puffy and his eyes are swollen. He looks like your typical drunk waking up from a vicious bender.

Before he has a chance to stand up I walk towards him and slap his face like an angry pimp with a back talking ho. It makes the sound of a frozen branch snapping under the weight of too much snow. His lips tremble with rage but his eyes resemble those of a whipped and spineless dog's. My gut says this expression is telling of the indecision inside his mind. To take his beating quietly or fight back? He chooses the latter.

"How's your old lady" he asks with a cruel grin?

"You leave her out of this" I say. "This is between you and me."

"I didn't bring her into this. You did."

"That's bullshit" I yell. "And if you hurt one hair on her head ever again I'll fucking kill you."

"It's up to you" he says still wearing that uppity smirk like an amateur poker player who thinks he's sitting on the winning hand. "You leave me alone and I leave her alone."

"You're fucking pathetic" I say. "Too weak to stand up to me man to man. You have to go behind my back and mess with my girl."

"This isn't about weakness. This is about survival. And I'm going to use every means possible."

"Listen Gerald" I scream. "You're not going to do shit to her."

"The hell I'm not" he says. "I'm staying alive. And if that's what it takes to get you to back down then so be it. You may be putting up a good fight but I'm the one in charge. I'm writing this fucking story. In fact this chapter's already done. And you don't know how it ends. For all you know Veronica's in trouble right now."

"I do to know how this chapter ends" I say. "It ends with me escaping from this stupid book you're writing. It ends with you disappearing forever. It ends with me taking over your life."

"I'm afraid I have different ending in mind" he says. "One that you might not like too much."

I take a moment and think. Weigh my options. Evaluate the scene. The son of a bitch has got me by the short and curlies. Or so he would like to think. But I'm not about to let some pencil dick putz strong arm me into submission. He says he'll hurt Veronica if I make a move. But who's to say he won't hurt her anyways. Who's to say he can be trusted at all. I decide the best thing to do is move on as planned.

"I think I like my ending better" I say.

Then I slap him again. And before he can respond I slap him once more even harder. Over and over until he finally rolls across the bed and makes a run for the door. I tackle him to the ground. He squirms like a child throwing a tantrum. I slip my arm around his neck from behind. Same shit as before. Just as I start choking him we disappear into one another.

It's even more vicious this time around. There's no warming up. No easing into it. No testing the water with our pinky toes. It's an all out free for all. An explosion of hatred and disgust. A battle in which the winner gets survival and the loser gets not a God damned thing but silence and darkness and oblivion.

And as if my own survival is not motivation enough I got the burden of Veronica's fate weighing on my shoulders like a thousand broken skies. What happens if I lose this fight? What lot will I have condemned her to? Will she die with me? Will she become Gerald's little voodoo doll? Will she get punished for my actions? Or will she become a widow? Forced to spend her remaining days alone and crazy with no one to share in the knowledge that she doesn't exist? And so I struggle on. Not only for me. For Veronica as well.

It's a strange way of fighting. We don't throw punches. We don't kick. We don't bite. We don't scratch. We don't strangle. We don't gouge. We don't pull out blades or chains or pistols. But somehow it's more violent than all that. It's more intense. More brutal. We fight with only our minds. We reduce the nature of conflict down to its most basic form. We concentrate our plights into two conflicting forces. No country. No flag. No name. No color. No shape. No cause save complete annihilation of that which opposes me. Just two crude masses struggling against the other.

We fight until our minds become delirious and weary. We fight until our souls begin to ache with pain. We fight until the walls of reality collapse and time starts acting cockeyed. Seconds are minutes. Minutes are hours. And hours stretch like enormous condoms.

Once again I'm overcome by exhaustion. I fight to hold on but eventually I succumb to the serenity that beckons from the darkness. When I wake up I'm lying on the floor of Gerald's bedroom. He wakes up at the same time. We look at each other for a moment. The room is silent and softly lit. I'm shocked to think that the afternoon has already arrived. But then he's on top of me. Clinging to me like a cheap suit. We wrestle around the room for a minute or two and then I get on top of him and pin him down. I start punching his face and then we're back inside his mind.

This cycle continues on into the evening. Bouts of vicious fighting divided by brief interludes in which we both catch our breath and rest or minds. Unlike last night I never truly gain the upper hand. We remain stalemated the entire time. Locked in a power struggle with a foe of equal strength and stamina.

At some point late in the night I wake up. The room is dark and my brain feels as if it's been ground into sausage then cooked over an open flame. It takes a great effort to sit up and look over at Gerald. He's awake. And not only is he watching me but he's sporting a twisted grin. A grin that disturbs me to the core. It seems to mock and pity me simultaneously.

I feel the rage burst from within me. I lunge onto him. But that's as far as it goes. I'm too weak to engage his mind. I'm unable to fight anymore. I've lost round three.

Feeling useless and scared I roll over and stare up at the ceiling. And this is when I remember Veronica Vaughn. My gut goes queasy. Fear grips my heart. Panic goes off in my head like an air raid siren.

Not knowing what else to do I struggle to my feet and hobble down the stairs. Behind me I can hear Gerald cackling like some windup Halloween doll. I run out through the front door and across the yard. I jump in the Caddy and fire it up then take off screeching through the nighttime streets.

Guilty thoughts torment my mind on the drive through town. They follow me. They trail me. They chase me like a pack of demon dogs sent to collect a soul that's bust loose from hell. I drive with my foot to the floor. I run reds. I fishtail every corner. But I can't escape. I can't shake loose the images of Veronica all alone and scared. I push my foot down even harder. I will the car through the dark and lifeless streets.

By the time I reach the apartment I'm a wreck. My hands are shaking. My palms are sweaty. My heart is racing. I can hardly work the front door key. Finally I get the door unlocked. I shove it open. I run up the stairs. I barge into our apartment.

"Veronica" I say as I stumble into the living room out of breath "I'm home. Are you all right babe?"

I walk through the apartment looking for her. She's nowhere to be seen. I call out her name. She doesn't answer. The radio in the living room is playing softly. I can hear the faint sound of Oscar Peterson tickling the ivories. I keep searching. Walking from room to room. Flipping on lights. Calling out her name. Looking for clues. Nothing. Nada. Zilch.

Frustration and worry grip my brain. I collapse onto the couch then pull out a Lucky and fire it up. I breathe the tobacco in deep. The smoke calms my nerves. I try to think straight. I try to form rational thoughts. I try to not lose it entirely. Where could she have gone? What could of happened to her? Is she injured? Is she dead? Or has she simply vanished? Just been erased from the story entirely? I take a deep drag and close my eyes.

Then I hear a sound coming from the front closet. The sound of someone crying. It startles me. I jump up and walk towards the closet.

"Veronica" I say in a scared and shaky whisper. "Is that you?"

"Don't look in here" comes the voice and I know it's her.

"What's going on" I ask? "Are you all right?"

"Just don't look in here" she says.

"Why not?"

"Because I don't want you to see me like this" she replies.

"What the fuck did he do to you" I demand as I pull open the door?

The closet is dark and it takes my eyes a moment to adjust. Even after they do I can't believe what I'm seeing. Crouched on the floor at the back of the closet is a disgusting mockery of all things human. A monster. A freak. A wretch. A hideous parody of what Veronica used to be.

Her face appears to have aged a thousand years. Boils and warts and whiskers cover her sagging flesh. What's left of her hair is grey and white and hangs from her scalp in thin clumps. Her mouth is nothing but a stinking hole of rot and decay. Gone are her pearly whites. Replaced by a few stained and crooked stumps. It looks like the mouth of a ninety year old who never brushed and whose diet consisted of nothing but Coca-Cola and Mars bars.

But worst of all is her body. It's covered with arms and legs. Limbs growing in all directions. Some small. Some large. Some appearing useful. Some just hanging worthless like overgrown peckers. Her clothing has been torn by the demands of her new body. I can see it all. Her breasts are grotesque and misshapen.

But despite the deformations it is still Veronica. Same voice. Same eyes. Same energy. This somehow makes it worse. I can't dismiss it as an abomination. I can't run out of the apartment screaming and vomiting. I can't kick it or punch it or slam the closet door in its face. I have to accept it for what it is. Veronica Vaughn. The woman I love.

Although she's reluctant I take one of her many hands and lead her out of the closet. She can't really walk. It's more of a crawl. A roll. A slither. She's ashamed of the way she looks. I'm ashamed of what I've done. And our accumulative shame looms over the both of us like a dark storm cloud. Underneath this cloud everything is heavy and somber and terrifying.

Not knowing what to say or do we turn off the lights and crawl into bed. I hold her freakish body next to mine and stare out the window into the night. It's not long before I start sobbing. And the last thing I feel before I cry myself into a troubled sleep is all her grotesque little hands trying lamely to wipe away the tears.

CHAPTER 17

▼

I STAND FOR A MOMENT AT THE EDGE LOOKING DOWN

Sometimes I wake up before my troubles do. I open my eyes. I smile up at the ceiling. And for a few moments everything is calm and simple and quiet. All the worries that plagued the previous day are still sleeping somewhere inside my mind.

But that's not the case this morning. This time my troubles aren't inside my head. They're laying next to me in the shape of a monster. A gray and sagging woman with a decaying mouth and a dozen useless limbs. And it's even worse than the night before. Something about the harsh morning light. The unforgiving brightness of the sun.

I stare across the pillow at Veronica's face. What's left of Veronica's face. I feel an anger inside me like a tumor. I'm beyond mad. Beyond pissed. Beyond fucking furious.

I pull the sheets back and rise from the bed. I'm already wide awake. I wash my face. I get dressed. I take my revolver from the dresser drawer. The drawer where it has laid dormant for months. Waiting for this reunion like a patient lover who hasn't moved on.

I hold it. Stare at it. Weigh it. It feels as if it doesn't belong in my hand. As if it belongs to a part of my life that has ended already. A part of my life that I can't reopen. A part of my life that is now obsolete. But it's not. And it never will be.

Guns aren't like hats or shoes or hair cuts. They aren't fashionable. They aren't trendy. They don't go out of style.

Then I see Veronica stirring under the covers. I turn and watch as she wakes up. I watch as she discovers her condition all over again. She lifts the blankets and looks down at her body. The tears pour from her eyes. But not me. I don't cry this morning. I'm too pissed to cry. And watching Veronica only flames my rage. I tuck the revolver in my waistband and keep getting ready.

"Please don't" she says through her tears.

"Don't what" I ask?

"Don't leave me."

"I have to get this straightened out."

"Please don't" she begs.

"I have to" I repeat.

"But I'm scared."

"Don't be" I say as I lean in and kiss her ancient and whiskery mouth. "This will all be over soon."

Then I jump in the Cadillac and lay a stretch of rubber. I skid to a stop in Gerald's driveway and take the front steps three at a time. The door hasn't been fixed so I just push it open and charge inside. I find him upstairs sound asleep in his bed.

"You're dead mother fucker" I say as I place the barrel of the revolver firmly against his forehead.

"Good morning to you too" he says.

"I told you what would happen if you hurt her."

"I guess I forgot" he says.

"You're acting awfully cute for someone whose brains are about to be all over their bedroom wall."

"Fuck you" he replies casually. "You're too much of a pussy to kill me."

"Is that so" I ask cocking the hammer?

"Damn right it is. And besides" he continues. "You should be grateful. Just think of the things she'll be able to do in the bedroom with all those little hands."

"That's it" I growl as I start to pull the trigger. "You're fucking dead."

But something doesn't feel right. Something's off. I have a hunch I'm being set up. This is when it hits me. He wants me to shoot him. I ease my finger off the trigger and think for a moment. Why would he want me to pop him? What does he gain if I blow his brains out? Then it clicks. If his character dies I have no way of taking over his mind. And if I can't take over the fictional Gerald I can't take over the real life Gerald. I'd be destroying the only exit I have. Then I'd be left in this bogus world forever. Trapped in this piece of shit mystery novel with a girlfriend that looks like a decaying octopus. And he'd be out there in the real world scott free. No longer in jeopardy of losing his mind to the character inside his book.

Hats off to Gerald. The son of a bitch is playing the Veronica card brilliantly. He has all the angles covered. But what he doesn't reckon on is me seeing through his little charade. But where does this leave me? What are my options now that I understand his game? It leaves me right back where I started. Trapped. Desperate. And with the fate of Veronica Vaughn weighing even heavier on my shoulders.

"Nice try" I say as I ease the hammer down and stick the gun back in my waistband.

"What are you talking about?"

"I'm talking about Veronica" I say. "I know what you're trying to do."

"I'm not trying to do anything" he says. "You're the one who's hurting her. And you're the one who can save her too. You just have to back off."

"I haven't done shit to her. And I never would. I love her."

"If you really love her" he says. "Then you'll back off. Because although it may not seem like it things can get a lot worse for her. A lot worse."

"Leave her the fuck alone" I demand.

"You leave me the fuck alone."

"Fuck you" I scream.

Then we get right down to it. I grab his mind with my own. I hammer away. I tear at his brain. I rip at his soul. I devour his identity. I try to get the upper hand right off the bat. And it works. I can tell that he's not ready for me. He's sluggish. He's groggy. He's surprised I didn't bite the bait and blow his head off. And I use this element of surprise to my advantage. I immediately find my way inside his mind. Deep inside his mind. I dig and thrash and kick and consume. I muscle my way inside his skull and begin to take it over.

I fight with a fury unmatched in any of our previous bouts. I fight for freedom. A freedom that I have never known. A life that I have never known. I fight for food and water and sex and fresh air and music and stars and cigarettes and all the other innumerable details that comprise real life. But I also fight for Veronica Vaughn. Knowing that her life is in my hands. Knowing her only hope for survival is that I win this battle.

And it appears as though I'm finally going to do so. I manage to stay on top of him. Keep him down. Keep the pressure on. But there's a certain part of him that

I can't get to. He keeps it blocked off. Hidden away. And so I keep chipping. Keep attacking. Keep working.

Fatigue settles in. I feel it in my brain. It's like a clamp tightening slowly on my skull. The pressure builds steadily. But I ignore it. I have to ignore it. I have no choice. To take even the slightest break could give Gerald the upper hand. And so I struggle onward. I push forward. I hold on for dear life.

Then the unthinkable happens. As my energy starts to fade I feel Gerald's start to build. We slowly switch roles. He attacks me. I go on the defense. I can feel his mind striking out. Hitting me. Dismantling me. Forcing me into a little box inside myself. I curl up and try my best to out last him.

Back and forth we go. Neither one willing to quit. Neither one willing to accept defeat. It turns into a bizarre dance. An ebb and flow. A war. A poem. An epic struggle of currents and energies and opposing forces. We revert back to the basics of survival. We lose ourselves in the blinding heat of combat.

I'm unable to judge the passing of time. Hours seem to race like clouds pushed by a mighty wind. But the next instant the wind stops and the hours seem to linger forever. Eventually I'm aware of the room becoming dark and I realize that night has come. Still we push on. On into the night. Into the darkness. Into the silent and eerie hours of early morning. Where lives are created and abandoned. Dreams shattered like frozen skulls. Fortunes found. Innocence lost. Tears shed. Teeth bared.

We remain stalemated. Remain locked in our strange and violent dance. Our minds mesh into one. Wrap around one another. Tighten like a coil. We dissolve under the pressure of the other one's attack. We dissect each other. We fade in and out of existence. We teeter on the brink of nothingness.

Then morning arrives. I'm lying in a heap by the side of the bed. It's the first time we've unlocked our minds since I arrived the previous morning. My body aches. My head throbs. My stomach growls. Then I see the face of Gerald Oscar Davidson looking down at me from the bed. He yells something I can't hear. I feel him fall on top of me. Then we're at it again.

This time it's a different sort of fight. We're both exhausted. Worn out. Ragged. Like two beat-up boxers hanging on to each other for dear life. Blood dripping. Arms heavy with fatigue. Eyes swollen shut. We lurch and stagger and throw big clumsy punches. We're both beyond the limits of our own understanding. We're battling on into unknown territory.

Filthy. Hideous. The fighting has regressed to something primal. Something bestial. Inside his mind is pure chaos. We both lose ourselves in the swirling disorder. We fight not only against each other but against madness itself.

Then it happens. My strength finally deserts me. I have nothing left. I feel Gerald taking over my mind. I feel my existence flicker like a flame in the wind. All of who I am begins to recede. My entire being turns to black and white.

I know in this instant that if I keep fighting I will lose. I will lose everything. Any chance of another fight. Any chance of becoming real. Any chance of saving Veronica. And so having no other options I'm forced to withdraw. I summon the last of my meager energy and in one final heave I disconnect my mind from Gerald's.

I wake up on the floor. The room is softly lit. Dawn is just around the corner. I'm coughing. I'm sick. I'm delirious. My body is tangled up with Gerald's. I stare up at the ceiling and try to focus myself. Basic questions flood my brain. Where am I? What day is it? Then I think of Veronica and everything comes back into focus. Everything becomes clear. Everything becomes urgent.

I untangle myself from Gerald and try to stand up. My knees buckle and I fall down. I try again and this time I succeed. I place my hand against the wall for support and slowly hobble out of the room. I fall at the bottom of the stairs. I get back up. I continue on.

The ride home is difficult. I'm fading in and out of consciousness. I swerve. I jump curbs. I bang into parked cars. But I keep moving forward. I force myself to keep driving. I'm propelled by the fear of what I might find. I'm propelled guilt. By shame. By love. By hope.

The apartment is silent. I can hear my heart hammering in my ears. I have a horrible feeling that I've made a huge mistake. On wobbly legs I walk through the apartment looking for Veronica.

I find her in the bedroom. She's still in bed. She's under the covers. I gently pull them back. She looks the same as when I left. And although it breaks my heart to see her like that I'm relieved nothing else has happened to her. But I don't even see her deformations. I don't see her flaws. All I see is Veronica Vaughn. The woman I love.

A wave of relief washes over me. I fall to my knees by the side of the bed. I look at her face. She's sound asleep. She looks peaceful. Content. Almost happy. I lean in and kiss her gently on the lips. Nothing else matters. We become as one. It's pure bliss. It's true passion. It's paradise.

But after a moment I realize she's not kissing me back. Her lips aren't moving. They're stiff. They're cold. They're rubbery. I open my eyes and look at her face. She hasn't woken up. She never will wake up. She's dead.

"No" I scream as I squeeze her with all my strength as if I believe I can somehow put her back together. "No. No. No."

Over and over and over. It's the only word my mind can grab a hold of. It pours out of me like blood. I shout it up into the heavens. I shout it down into hell. I shout it everywhere. I fill the entire world with my horrible cry. I scream until there's nothing left in me. Until all of who I am is sent out to scour the earth for redemption.

I wake up the following morning starving but well rested. I'm lying on the floor holding one of Veronica's many dead hands in mine. It's stiff and feels like a mannequin's hand. I stand up and walk into the kitchen where I commence to raid the fridge of everything edible. After I'm done with the fridge I open the cupboards and eat some more.

When I can't fit any more in my stomach I walk into the bathroom and crawl into the shower. The hot water is soothing on my sore and tired muscles. I sit down in the tub and let the water fall all over me. I breathe in the steam. I drink the water. I melt into the tub.

After the shower I get dressed and wrap Veronica's body up in a sheet. I carry her outside and dump her in the trunk of my Cadillac. Next I hit a hardware store on the south side of town. I pick up a nice sturdy shovel. Then I get on the highway and head out into the country.

I flip on the radio and fire up a Lucky. A sad calmness settles over me. A feeling of emptiness. Of bitter acceptance. I breathe the smoke in as deep as it will go then blow it out nice and slow. I can hear Barbara Carroll on the radio jamming on the piano. She's covering a tune called "Goodbye." It seems a fitting number so I turn it up loud.

Off to my right I can see the Mississippi River. It looks like a solid path of silver. Like you could drive your car right up the middle of it and never know about all the trash hiding under the surface. It seems symbolic of life in general. The way people can seem so shinny and bright while beneath the surface dark currents flow and drag dirty secrets through the muck and slime.

Then they play a Red Norvo Jam. The song's titled "The One That Got Away." It too is a fitting number. I light another smoke with the butt of the first. The tobacco tastes stale and old. The Caddy charges down the road. The rain clouds up above get even darker. The Mississippi keeps swerving right along with me. And I'm lost in a quiet world of melancholy thoughts.

Eventually I reach my destination. The place where Veronica and I made love in the back seat of the Cadillac. That afternoon seems like a lifetime ago. Back when she was still singing. Back when I was just a fellow fresh out the war with the whole world in front of me. Back when we both thought we actually existed. Back when everything simple and cool.

I park my car. I pop the trunk. And there under the dark autumn sky I start digging my true love's grave. I quickly fall into a frantic rhythm. I dig as though I've not come here to leave something. But rather to look for something I've lost. And maybe there's some truth to that. Maybe I have lost something along the way. Some part of myself that I've unknowingly sacrificed for my obsession. Some part of myself that I can never get back no matter how deep I dig.

When I'm done shoveling I pick up Veronica's body from the trunk and carry her to the hole. I stand for a moment at the edge looking down. And this is when it all hits home. This is when it becomes real. This is when the magnitude of what's happened falls from the sky like a screaming nightmare and hits me right between the eyes.

Part of me wants to join her. To call it quits. To climb down into the hole beside her and bury my face in the grime. To close my eyes once and for all and empty my heart of all the pain and shit that's accumulated there. I want to crawl into the ground and eat the dirt and the mud. I want to become the earth. I want to rot alongside Veronica so that someday we might dissolve into one and sprout up from the soil in the shape of a single tree.

And that's what I do. I crawl down into the muddy grave and hold the deformed body of my dead girlfriend. And as my tears begin to fall so does the rain. They mix together. They become one. Until the sky itself begins to cry. Until the earth begins to weep. Until Veronica and I are just a couple of nameless corpses drowning in heaven's tears.

CHAPTER 18

▼

A VOICE LIKE A SEX KITTEN ANGEL ON A COUPLE OF DOWNERS

Men fight for many different reasons. Some fight to protect their country. Some fight over women. Some fight over turf. Some fight over food. And some just fight when they're drunk and pissed at the world and need to blow steam. There's a lot of different reasons. But there's always one common thread. They fight because there's something they got that they don't want to lose. Their girl. Their reputation. Their freedom. Their life.

But what compels a man to fight when he's got nothing left to lose? He fights because he no longer cares. He fights because it's the first time in his God damned life that he's got the upper hand. He fights because he's been whipped so long that the pain has become a close friend. Because he is now like the rain in the gutter. He is the sawdust on the floor of the saloon. He is the dried-up blood on the edge of society's blade. He is a rat with broken teeth gnawing on a piece of gristle. He knows nothing about nothing. He could give two shits. He could give a flying fuck. He fights because he has one last chance to bite off the hand of the person who beat him. He fights because the whole world is one big fight and he wants to get in on the action.

This is me. This is my state. I've got nothing left. I've been robbed blind. Chewed on. Coughed up. Spit out. Left on the dirty sidewalk like glob of lung cheese. A broken cigarette. An empty booze bottle. A cum-filled rubber. I've been stripped bare. No woman. No pride. No life. Nothing save the desire to take Gerald with me on a trip to the outskirts of nowhere. I want to drag him down into the pits of oblivion. I want to turn the tables on this cocksucker and let him know how it feels to have someone else calling the shots. I want to destroy my maker and see what exists on the other side of creation.

I pull up out front of Gerald's place later in the evening. My head is as empty as a ghost town. My heart is a tattooed fist. My soul is a cold chiseled dagger. My entire bullshit existence comes down to one final show down. I step out of the Caddy and walk up the driveway.

It's dark out. There's a harsh fall wind whipping through the trees. The leaves shake and rustle and seem to whisper something I can't understand. The streetlights flicker lamely as if they too are trying to tell me something. The entire neighborhood is struggling to convey a message. Some message I'll never understand. Some message I don't give a rat's ass about anyways.

Gerald's door is still busted. I push it open and walk inside. I find him in the den. Just sitting there waiting as if he knew I was coming. Which I'm sure he did. I take a seat opposite the couch and stare him straight in the eyes. We don't say anything. We don't need to. We both know that words don't mean shit. We both know that this is our last meeting. That things are getting settled come hell or high water.

But there's something else. A duality. An overlapping. A mirror image. A mutual climax. My entire hogwash life is coming to a peak. As is Gerald's novel. And because of this we're both connected. We're linked. We're interwoven. My existence. His work. The two have become one. And we know that the time has come for all scores to get settled.

And so we get down to it. Not franticly. Not violently. No screaming. No yelling. No punching. We simply stare into each other's eyes. We stare until we begin to fade into one. Like two old sailors setting out to sea. We stand on the deck and watch the shore recede into nothing. Knowing that this is our last voyage. Knowing that we will never set foot on land again. And if we do it will not be as we remembered it.

It begins as a shoving. A slow and steady thrust. Our identities heaving against one another. But it's still not violent. Not savage. It's a battle as slow and natural as water against rock. A river winding its way through the land. Waves crashing against the shore. Rain hammering the earth.

But even nature can become violent. The planets can align. The Gods can get angry. Time can stack up like a pile of nudey mags in a young boy's clubhouse. Until eventually something gives. The earth rumbles. The winds howl. The sky becomes black. The rains come and wipe away all life. This is the case with Gerald and I. Our slow and deliberate battle gradually becomes a storm.

It builds slowly. Like black thunder clouds rolling over the horizon. Then there's a flash of lightning. A blast of thunder. The wind gusts down and bites into my bones. The clouds are above me and everything is dark. The first few drops tap at the soil. The rain falls from the sky with a heartless fury. The entire universe screams down upon me.

And so it begins. All the speeches and dumb ass rallies have ended. The marching is over. The drums are done beating. The smoke has cleared. And there's nothing left but a battlefield. An enemy. A war cry. Then the sound of crashing metal and blood spilling onto the ground.

At first I'm able to judge the passing of time. The never-ending night. With it's bleak and desperate hours. Then the morning comes. Light spilling over the streets like sweet wine. The slow rebirth of a world that's cursed to die over and over. The day fades into purple twilight. Evening becomes night. Until once again I lose my grip on reality and I'm sucked into the void of inner space.

I'm inside Gerald's mind. I am Gerald's mind. His skull is a cage and I'm the prisoner. But there's someone else in here with me. Something else locked up beside me. It's dark. I can't see. But I can feel its presence. We're circling each other. A couple of dogs sniffing each other's assholes. Paranoid cellmates with nigger-rigged shivs.

We piss to mark our spot. We curl a lip and show our fangs. We pull a deep growl out of our throats and shove it in the other one's face. Nothing works. And so we jump on the other one. Sink our teeth into their flesh. Taste their blood. Rip. Bite. Shred. And then there's a hurting in my gut. A snap of fangs in my face. A moment of red. The entire stinking universe shuts down in the blink of hummingbird's eye and I lose all reality as I know it.

Then it's back. But it's blurred. It's diluted and filthy. The river of my identity has been polluted with trash. Someone's been shitting upstream. Dumping their thoughts into the water. Pouring out buckets of memories that aren't mine. It's everywhere. Swirling around inside me. Engulfing me. I see a childhood that's fraudulent. Con artists. Strangers. Siblings that aren't mine. Parents that I've never seen before staring at me with empty eyes.

There's more and more. It's all I can see. It's all like one long lucid nightmare. Each image is wrong. In contradiction of all that I am. They disturb me to the core. They rot my soul. They devour my life. They make me sick and chuckle while I drown in my own vomit. And there's a pulling at my feet. Something's dragging me down. Then I'm sucking in rancid water. I can't breathe. There's a burning in my chest. My essence is shrinking like a solitary snowflake in a sidewalk puddle.

But I see a memory that's mine. It saves me. It's of gal I used to roll around with. Met her in a swanky jazz bar down south. Had a voice like a sex kitten angel on a couple of downers. A body that could strut down the sidewalk like a one-person parade. Long legs. Round ass. Perfect tits. She had it all. And a little extra stashed in a shoe box back home under her bed. We're sharing a joint in the alley behind the club where she worked. She's laughing out loud and hanging all over me and I'm hanging on to her. Her leg lifts. The dress comes up. My hand slides over her garter. There's a flash of smooth skin. Breath in my ear. Then straight up joy as I tilt my head back and look up into the starry summer night. Her name is Veronica Vaughn. She used to love me. And I know this memory is mine. It has to be. It's all I've known. It's all I have. It's who I am.

More follow. I see family members. I feel emotions. I recall apartments that I rented. Cars I drove. Guys whose asses I kicked. Teachers I had a crush on.

Memories fall down on my dried out mind. It absorbs it like thirsty soil drinks the rain after a cruel drought. And in this downpour of life I see more images of Veronica. I remember how much I love her.

I feel my identity surge. I believe in life. I believe that I deserve to be free. To bow to no man. To bend over for nothing and for nobody. To feel pain. Sorrow. Joy. Pride. Hunger. Satisfaction. All of it. To pursue a life that I'm entitled to. A reality that I have a right to experience. Good or bad. Just something that's real.

Back and forth we go. Like a couple of special kids on a teeter-totter who don't know how to stop. Because the river runs forever. Because there's no ending. And the water coughs in the crap. The water chokes and spits. The water struggles to keep the pollution out. But the pollution struggles to keep the water out.

And the whole God damned thing is just a churning mass of chaos. A river of madness and screaming voices. The pulp of two smashed and ruined lives mixed up together as one and dumped into a cocktail glass. Everything I've accepted as reality is boiled down into nothing. Reduced to the minimum.

Numbers. Shoes. Erections. Wall paper. Jazz music. Candle wax. Cheap whiskey. Chinese soup. Highways. Automatic riffles. Petting parties. Movies. Novels. Pussies. Malt shops. Pool halls. Christmas trees. Crowbars.

Everything melts into the same thing. My entire consciousness becomes one. One sound. One color. One idea.

Tire swings. Lipstick. Cartoons. Funerals. Sunsets. Teddy bears. Blowjobs. Surfboards. Fist fights.

But it keeps shrinking until I have nothing at all. Then I have less than nothing. I have an emptiness that keeps spreading. A hole in my head and everything is falling out. My skull is draining like a tub with the plug pulled.

Life. Acceptance. Boxcars. Churches. Meaning. Understanding. Switchblades.

I'm fighting off the darkness. And I'm in the freezing cold center of pure nothingness. Drifting into a million different pieces. Floating weightless and free like a deserted world on the other side of the universe.

Awareness. Joy. Dump trucks. Fishing holes.

I keep fighting. But for what? I don't know. And the darkness is scary.

Birth. Death. Slingshots.

I'm not real. I don't exist.

Sin.

Keep fighting.

Beer.

What does it all mean?

Hell.

I'm not real. I'm a phony. My thoughts are phony. Words are phony. Everything's phony.

Bus stations.

I love Veronica Vaughn.

Truth.

It's silent. It's peaceful. I don't know where I am.

Jukebox.

And my Mom and Dad don't know where I am. And nobody knows where I am.

Briefcase.

I'm completely gone. It doesn't hurt. It doesn't feel like anything at all. And the music stops. And the lights go out for good. And everyone leaves the auditorium.

Everything is everything. And everything is empty.

Then I see the darkness spread and the sky opens up and the light comes shining in and I spread my wings and fly upwards into the blinding heat of absolute reality.

I'm embraced.

I'm loved.
I'm home.
I'm done.
I'm nothing.
Who would be born must first destroy a world.
The bird flies to God.

PART IV

CHAPTER 19

▼

EASTBOUND IN A LONG BLACK CADILLAC

I woke up in some downstairs office. I was slumped over a desk with my face on a typewriter. I couldn't recall for the life of me how I got there. I was confused and disoriented and the more I tried to figure it out the less it made sense. I sat up slowly and looked around the room. Everything was blurry and out of focus. It felt like I was three sheets to the wind.

I must of sat there for an hour. Beating up my brain. Working it over. Pounding it like a hired goon with a steel pipe. Nothing came to me. It was as though I had been born at that moment and was trying to recall details to a past that had never actually happened.

Eventually my confusion became dizzying and I felt my stomach start tightening up on me. I stumbled from the chair and ran out of the room looking for the john. I found one in the hallway and barged in just as my innards came shooting out of my mouth.

After I was done I knelt there for a while. It was quiet and I found the cool tile floor to be soothing. Then I pulled myself up onto my feet and stepped over to the sink to splash some cold water on my face.

It was then that everything came back to me. For just as I finished washing my face I caught my reflection in the mirror. It was Gerald Oscar Davidson. I couldn't believe my eyes. I stumbled backwards in shock. It was me. And yet it wasn't.

I leaned in close to the mirror and ran my brand new hands over my brand new face. It was a strange feeling. Almost as if I was wearing a costume. Almost as if I was trespassing in a stranger's home. I stood there staring at my reflection and feeling a million different emotions at once.

I walked back into Gerald's study and looked for a pack of smokes. I found some and lit one up. It wasn't a Lucky. It was a Pall Mall. But I didn't give a shit. It was my fist real cigarette and that was good enough for me.

It was after the cigarette as I sat at Gerald's desk with my feet kicked up that reality cold cocked me a good one and the tears started falling like a hard rain. I cried for every reason there is to cry. And a few others I made up myself. I cried from exhaustion. I cried from joy. I cried from fear. But mostly I cried because I knew I had blown it big time by losing Veronica. I closed my eyes and fell into a dark lonely sleep.

The next two weeks passed in a fog of grief and cheap whiskey. I'd chain-smoke cigarettes and wander the halls of a house that wasn't mine. I'd walk past mirrors and catch glimpses of a stranger staring back at me. I'd sit in Gerald's study drinking booze and flipping through his unfinished manuscript in search of something I couldn't put my finger on. I'd spend entire days just reading the same sex scene over and over. I'd wake up some nights soaked in sweat and screaming Veronica's name into the darkness.

I went for drives into the country and drank coffee in roadside dives. I sat alone in dark smoky bars tossing back shots of liquor and feeding coins into melancholy jukeboxes. I walked the sidewalks at night and smoked cigarettes under the November rain. I stopped at nightclubs and stared through the windows at the jazzmen with their cool shades and shinny trumpets. Then I'd turn up my collar and keep walking on down the line.

Everything I did was just a distraction. Everything thing I did was in vain. Everything I did was just piss in the wind. I tried to convince myself that it was worth it. That reality was a kick in the pants and that life was nothing but peaches and cream. But it wasn't true. There's as much bullshit in reality as there is truth in fiction. And at least inside the book I had a good dame to call my own.

And so I numbed the pain with gin and jazz music. With cigarettes and memories. I wallowed in self-pity and played the roll of the guilt ridden looser. It wasn't the roll I wanted but it beat not being on the stage at all. So I played the part as best as I could. I pouted. I cursed. I withdrew. I spent my nights crying in front of the bedroom mirror and watching tears roll down a stranger's face.

Then one day I was moping around Gerald's study and came across some photos tucked away in a desk drawer. My jaw dropped as I realized they were the same pictures as the ones in the manuscript. I quickly shuffled through them until I found the ones of Veronica. Standing behind the counter of some beat New York diner. Holding a pen and a flip pad and staring off into nowhere like a sleepy child searching for a dream that upped and vanished in the middle of the night.

And as I stared at the images of Veronica a detail caught my eye. In the background was a couple of small beat-up street signs. With my heart beating like a jazz drummer loaded on moonshine and Benzedrine I frantically searched the desk for a magnifying glass. I found one and held it over the photo. The diner was on the corner of Bleecker Street and Seventh Avenue.

I sat the magnifying glass down then leaned back in the chair and closed my eyes. I couldn't believe I hadn't thought of it sooner. I could drive to New York. I could find the diner. I could find the real life Veronica Vaughn. I could at least see if there was anything there.

It was a long shot. But all good things are long shots. Nothing comes easy in this crazy world. And it's only when the stakes are high that the payoff is sugar sweet. That's why it's always cooler when the underdog wins. When the little fellow whips the big guy's ass. When the no name horse comes from out of nowhere. When the scrawny four-eyed punching bag finally blows his top and gives the bully what for. Because life isn't like the movies. You're not going to get a Hollywood ending unless you put your pecker on the line. Unless you put the chips on the table and call the other guy's bluff.

The next week was a blur of wild and impulsive behavior. First I made some quick phone calls and got the skinny on Gerald's financial situation. Then I got to work liquidating his funds and by the end of the week I was sitting on a shit ton of cash. The house. The car. The stocks. The bonds. The savings. The checking. The inheritance. You name it and I got money for it. Every God damned thing I could get my greasy mitts on.

"Are you sure this is what you want to be doing" Gerald's lawyer asked while I sat in his office signing papers? "This all just seems a little rushed. A little crazy."

"Shit man" I said with a smile. "You don't got the foggiest idea how crazy this is."

The next day I went to a used car lot and paid cash for a black 1946 Cadillac. It was the same car I drove in the manuscript and it felt nice to get it back. I rolled across town and made one last stop by the house. The place was empty. The Salvation Army had come by the day before and cleared out all the rooms.

All the rooms except for the study. And that's the room I headed for. I opened the stash box in the wall and removed two briefcases. One of which contained the money. And the other contained the manuscript. I loaded them both in my Caddy and took off toward the highway.

And so I split Shreveport about the same way I rolled in. Eastbound in a long black Cadillac. But there's one big difference. I arrived running away from life. I left running toward it. When I blew into Shreveport I had nothing but a past full of haunted memories. When I left I had no past at all.

All I had was a sweet ride and a full tank of gas. All I had was a fresh pack of smokes and a keen appreciation of what it means to be alive. All I had was two strong hands and a love for a woman I had never even met. All I had was the future. And the future was a flower blossoming for the first time under the warm watchful eye of the morning sun.

CHAPTER 20

▼

THE WORLD WAS ALIVE
AND SO WERE WE

After a couple days on the road I rolled into New York on a Wednesday night around the first of December. An early winter storm was just hitting the city and the sky was thick with snowflakes. They floated as weightless as dandelion tufts on a summer breeze. I just eased it along nice and slow. Smoking like a chimney and listening to Duke Ellington on a jazz station I found coming through Jersey.

Then I saw Manhattan emerge from out of the storm. The buildings were all lit up and looked like roman candles reaching fiery fingers into the snowy night. They seemed to glow like a holy mirage. They beckoned me into their world of romance and wonder.

I crossed over the George Washington Bridge then hit a gas station and bought a map of the city. I found where Bleecker Street hit Seventh Avenue. I tucked the map in the glove box. I pulled back out into traffic.

I jumped onto Broadway and took it all the way down the length of Manhattan. It was slow going. But I enjoyed the show. I had never seen anything so strange and magical as New York City at night with the snow coming down.

The city is a civilization all its own. The city is a poem chiseled in stone. The city is an entity that feeds on the dreams of all those who inhabit it. And as I drove through the crowded neon streets I understood how people could live their entire lives and want for nothing more than to remain anonymous and safe within the womb of that bleak and noble metropolis.

I saw a black lady bundled up to her eye balls dragging her kids along the sidewalk toward the subway entrance. I saw a couple of sweet-faced teenage girls with gloves and matching earmuffs trying to catch snowflakes on their tongues. I saw a street vendor slinging sausages and kraut despite the weather. I saw a line of cabs a mile long stretching down Broadway like a shiny yellow snake. I saw Times Square with all the theatre marques flashing like a lightening storm. I saw wide-eyed tourists cuddling under a blanket in the back of a horse pulled carriage. I saw a city smiling brilliantly in the middle of its own evolution.

When I hit Fourteenth Street I hung a right and cut over to Greenwich Avenue. This put me smack dab in the middle of the Village. Hipsters and babes ran hand in hand through the bustling intersections. Longhaired intellectuals held books under their arms and smoked nervously while waiting for the bus. Bars and coffee shops lined the streets and laughter could be heard pouring out onto the sidewalk.

Then I was on the corner of Bleecker and Seventh. And sure enough. There it was. Just like in the picture. It was called the Bleecker Street Cafe. Just a run of the mill diner with an awning over the front door and a neon sign up above.

I parked my Cadillac then dashed across the snow-covered street and into the diner. A bell rang when I opened the door but no one bothered to look up. To my left there was a young fellow with his nose stuck in a paperback drinking a cup of coffee. To my right was a workingman a little older than myself digging into some chicken fried steak. In the booth behind him were some college kids sharing a piece of pie and working on a round of beers.

I parked myself at the counter and lit my last cigarette. Then a heavyset guy with a bald head came lumbering out of the kitchen. He was wearing checkered pants and a white T-shirt with a greasy apron hanging around his meaty neck. He looked like one of those guys that used to be hot shit back in the day but didn't age so well over the years. Now he just busts his hump for peanuts and tries to forget about all the times the cards didn't fall his way.

"What'll it be tonight" he asked as he ran a rag over the red Formica counter top?

"Actually I'm not too hungry" I said. "I was just hoping to ask you a question."

"What about" he asked and lost what little smile there had been on his whiskery face?

"About a gal that works here. I was just wondering if you could tell me when she might be in next."

"What's her name" he asked with distrust in his bloodshot eyes?

"See that's the thing" I said. "I don't exactly know."

"How you want me to tell you when she works next if you don't even know who she is?"

"You'll know who I'm talking about" I said. "They don't make too many look like her. She's about five seven with light brown hair. Gorgeous face and has a body like a pinup girl."

"Sorry pal" he said as he took another swipe with the rag. "She quit a while back."

"You're kidding me" I mumbled as I leaned back and let it sink in?

"Nope."

"Well what's her name" I asked in desperation?

"I'm not saying."

"Why not?"

"Because I don't know you from Adam" he said setting his rag down and staring me square in the eyes. "That's why not."

"I'm not a nut or something if that's what you're thinking. I just want to talk to her."

"I gave you my answer" he said folding his arms and resting them on his beer belly. "Now beat it."

"Would it make a difference if I told you it wasn't even me who wanted to meet her? It was a buddy of mine."

"Oh really" he said shifting all his bulk to one side. "And who might that be?"

"It might be my friend Hamilton" I said slipping a ten spot out of my wallet and setting it on the counter.

He looked from side to side before letting his eyes land on the money. Indecision crossed his face and he shifted nervously back and forth. Then he picked up his rag and started wiping the counter again.

"Sorry" he said. "But I've heard about that Hamilton guy. I don't care for him much."

"Did I say Hamilton? I'm sorry. I meant my friend Jackson" and I put a twenty on top of the ten.

"Her name's Anastasia" he said in a low voice while he slipped the bills in his pocket. "Anastasia Heartly."

"And where can I find her" I asked?

"I bump into her from time to time at a coffeehouse down the street. Little place called Jimmy's on the corner of Bedford and Seventh."

"Was that so hard" I asked then put my cigarette out in the ashtray and headed for the door?

I came across Jimmy's in no time flat. It was a dumpy looking joint but that didn't seem to hurt business. People were all over the sidewalk. Some coming. Some going. Some just standing around smoking and digging the crazy weather.

I cut through the cluster of hipsters and made my way inside. The place was dark and laidback. Cool cats sat around smoking hand rolled cigarettes and listening to jazz. Students lounged on sofas and philosophized about life and art. Some guy with a dragon tattoo on his forearm sat on a bean bag and played chess with a cute young gal with ponytails and freckles.

I bellied up to the counter and ordered a cup of coffee. I doctored it up with cream and sugar then went looking for a seat. That's when I saw her. She was sitting alone in the corner reading a book. She was even more stunning than I remembered. It took all my strength to not run over and pick her up and twirl her around the room.

She was wearing a pair of pinstriped slacks with an off-white blouse tucked in at the waist. It wasn't a flattering getup. But it didn't need to be. Any man with an ounce of gumption left in him could see the potential of what was hiding inside. Her hair was a little shorter than I remembered. A little blonder too. The light fell just right and made it sparkle with hints of gold. But other than that she was exactly the same. Same full lips. Same sultry eyes. Same drop dead body.

"This seat belong to anybody" I asked pointing to the chair next to her?"

"I don't see anybody's name on it."

I took a seat and played it cool. I drank my coffee. I listened to all the people talking and laughing. I watched the snow falling outside the window. I checked her out of the corner of my eye and tried to think of something to say. I smelt her perfume and thought about how nice it would be to touch her.

"Cigarette" I asked finally?

"I've got my own" she replied without looking up.

"I mean can I get one? I'm all out."

"I guess" she replied coldly then reached into her purse and handed me a Camel.

"Can I get a light" I asked?

"What do you want me to smoke it for you too?"

"Sorry" I said and leaned back in my chair like a whipped dog thinking maybe this whole thing was a bad idea.

"I'm sorry too" she said leaning over and lighting my cigarette. "I shouldn't be taking my shitty day out on you."

"Don't worry about it" I said. "And thanks for the cigarette."

"Hey" she said looking at me kind of funny. "Have we met before? Your face looks familiar."

"I don't think so" I said. "But I knew a fellow lived in this neighborhood looked a lot like me. Maybe you saw him."

"Maybe" she said.

"My name's Buckley by the way."

"Anastasia" she said shaking my hand.

"So what are you reading Anastasia" I asked?

"Narcissus and Goldman" she replied.

"That's Herman Hesse right?"

"You know Herman Hesse?"

"Not personally" I said. "But I like his work."

"Smartass" she said with a sly smile. "But seriously. You've read some Hesse?"

"Only Demian. But I enjoyed it."

"That's cool" she said. "It's not everyday you meet someone who's read Hesse. He's probably my favorite writer."

"Why's that" I asked?

"Because of the way he makes me feel" she said. "It might sound stupid but there's something about his words that help me understand who I am. Whenever I read one of his books I feel as though I've come closer to figuring out what I'm supposed to be doing with my life."

"That doesn't sound stupid at all" I said as I put my cigarette out in the ashtray. "In fact I couldn't agree with you more. I wouldn't be the man I am today if I hadn't read Demian."

"You want another one" she asked reaching into her purse?

"Why not?"

"I think I'll join you this time" she said fishing a couple more Camels out of her purse.

"Thanks" I said and lit both of our cigarettes.

"I thought you didn't have a lighter."

"I did" I said. "I just wanted to talk to you a little longer."

We smoked for a couple minutes without saying anything. We loosened up. We felt at ease. We people watched and enjoyed the scene. We peeked at each other and tried not to get caught.

"So why are you so into literature" she asked blowing out a mouthful of smoke? "You a student around here?"

"No" I said. "I've just always liked reading. I also write some."

"What do you write" she asked?

"I'm working on a novel."

"Really?"

"Really" I said. "In fact I moved here to New York to finish it."

"When was that" she asked?

"About twenty-five minutes ago" I said with a grin and we both started laughing.

"And what's your novel about" she asked?

"You wouldn't believe me if I told you."

"Try me" she said.

"All right. But what do you say we blow this joint and I tell you about it over a couple of cold beers?"

"You're on" she replied.

We grabbed our coats and stepped outside into the stormy night. Into a city as glorious as any dream I had ever had. Into a life that I had to fight like hell to get. I put my arm around Anastasia to keep her warm. She didn't pull away. The world was alive and so were we.

978-0-595-35048-3
0-595-35048-8

32070263R00100

Made in the USA
San Bernardino, CA
10 April 2019